ELVES WAR-FIGHTING MANUAL

Also by Den Patrick:

Orcs War-Fighting Manual
Dwarves War-Fighting Manual

ELVES

WAR-FIGHTING MANUAL

Den Patrick

Illustrations by Andrew James

GOLLANCZ
LONDON

The right of Den Patrick to be identified
as the author of this work has been asserted by him in
accordance with the Copyright, Designs and Patents Act 1988.

First published in Great Britain in 2013 by Gollancz
An imprint of the Orion Publishing Group
Orion House, 5 Upper St Martin's Lane, London WC2H 9EA
An Hachette UK Company

A CIP catalogue record for this book is available
from the British Library

ISBN 978 0 575 13277 1

1 3 5 7 9 10 8 6 4 2

Typeset at The Spartan Press Ltd,
Lymington, Hants

Printed and bound in Great Britain by
Clays Ltd, St Ives plc

The Orion Publishing Group's policy is to use papers that
are natural, renewable and recyclable products and made
from wood grown in sustainable forests. The logging and
manufacturing processes are expected to conform to the
environmental regulations of the country of origin.

www.orionbooks.co.uk
www.gollancz.co.uk

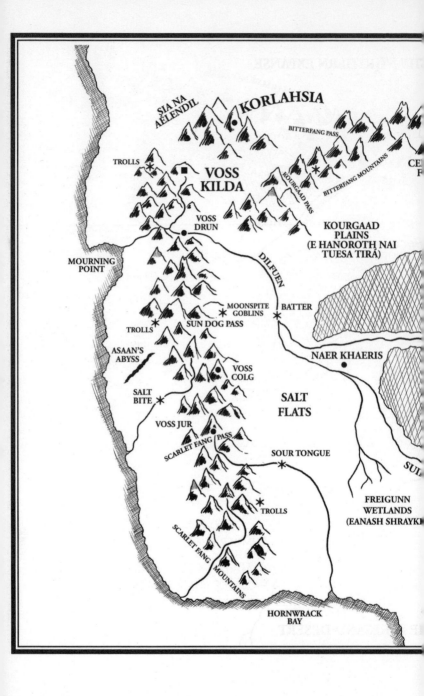

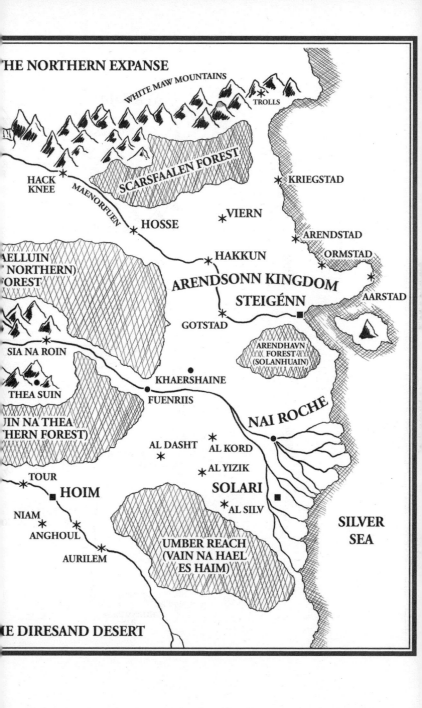

THE AELFIR ART OF WAR

I

WAR IS THE ONLY CONSTANT

We *aelfir*, eldest of the races, most fair, abundantly benevolent, and wise beyond the limited imagining of lesser minds, have much to be grateful for. Due to the immeasurable span of our lives we have come to know and master many disciplines. Khaeris herself spent over a thousand years bringing knowledge to our people. Our craftsmanship is the most envied in the world; we can work miracles of design and practicality in wood and metal, leather and cloth. Our diplomats have negotiated the apparently impossible, averting bloodshed when all seemed lost. With Khaeris' teaching we can step out from death's shadow and can reverse the gravest of illnesses. And yet there is one arena for which Khaeris did not instruct us.

War.

Few things are as inevitable as war. The seasons drift from pleasant and mild to dreadful and cruel. Rains cause rivers to burst their banks, and crops are blighted by frost and pests. Volcanoes belch and spew fiery chaos across the land, and fell winds arrive from the south-east, tearing up towns and trees. Beauty fades, love dies and even the stars themselves dwindle in time.

ᴛʜᴇ ᴀʀᴛ ᴏꜰ ᴡᴀʀ

Naer Evain, for all its breathtaking beauty, is a place of constant friction and disharmony. Even we *aelfir* can be obliged to resort to physical intervention. 'Violence is the last refuge of the incompetent' is often quoted in the royal courts, but what use are pretty quotes when the orcs bring their barbed spears? And what use a bright and brilliant mind when the dwarves seek only to hammer our brains from our skulls?

Pacifist poets and artists who blanch at the sight of a blade will ask, 'Can we not negotiate with the younger races?' This thinking is as ridiculous as it is infantile. Orcs constantly seek to expand their borders; they nurture an implacable hatred for the chosen of Khaeris. The dwarves covet our knowledge and begrudge our communion with the land and the forests. The humans spread like weeds, threatening to overrun Naer Evain with total lack of care. These are the factors that must bring the younger races into conflict with the *aelfir*.[1]

1 *The* Aelfir *Art of War* was originally penned in a period called the Reunification, before humans came down from the Northern Expanse. The Reunification lasted two hundred and twenty years. This translation is from an edition revised and released during an era the *aelfir* call the Shadow War, which occurred nearly a thousand years later. I still struggle to comprehend how old La Darielle Daellen Staern really is.

Lately we have witnessed a greater threat: a darkness rises in Umber Reach that casts its shadow across the land. Every living thing has much to fear from the *Hael Es Haim*.[2] It is bad enough they come to our homes under the cover of darkness and prey on the innocent; yet rumours and reports would confirm that the *Hael Es Haim* seek to stir up conflict between all the races. Orcs are continually encouraged and goaded into mindless acts of savagery by their shamans. The same shamans make allies of the once feral *akuun*, imbuing them with obedience and purpose.[3] Sly humans, so-called alchemists, seek to bargain with powers beyond their meagre comprehension. They sell their souls to the *Hael Es Haim* in exchange for some agenda even we *aelfir* cannot guess at. The goblins too, ever the most pitiful and lacklustre of the races, possibly even more so than the humans, have stumbled across their own petty magics. It is unquestionable that the root of this new power lies in the shadows of Umber Reach.

We live in a time when all races on Naer Evain have the potential to threaten the *aelfir*'s arcane dominance. This, over time, could lead to our extinction.

It is for this reason that I am setting down my thoughts here, so that future generations may benefit

2 *Hael Es Haim* translates as 'one whose shadow is clouded with fury'. This term is also used for the creatures which inhabit Umber Reach, and the entities that human alchemists and orc shamans summon.

3 *Akuun* is the word for troll. Curiously the *aelfir* do not have their own word and use a word borrowed from the orc language. This is highly unusual, as the *aelfir*'s disdain of the other races and their languages is legendary.

from what I have learned during my short span.[4] In this volume I hope to make a study of every weapon at our disposal, the units of troops we use and why we use them. I will explain what armour a warrior should wear for which mission, and the best uses for cavalry. It is my wish to make clear our most trusted tactics and also to educate on the subjects of terrain and philosophy. Either of these may be a warrior's greatest ally but just as easily turn treacherous if we are not mindful of them.

All I have known is war. My parents were slain during an orc Harrowing that saw half of Naer Khaeris left in ruins. I was raised under a shroud of smoke with the scent of blood on the air. I had already mastered the Breath when most *aelfir* are learning Treesinging. I was the youngest *aelfir* to graduate from the Haimkor Sword School. I have ridden against the orcs with Sight and Indignation; served with the *Drae Adhe*, ambushing pale humans. It was my privilege and greatest honour to serve in the High King's retinue.[5] I have hunted dwarves at the Siege of Korlahsia and been decorated with the blood of my enemies. I trained at Kaershåine, taught at Sia Na

4 La Darielle Daellen Staern wrote the original draft of *The* Aelfir *Art of War* when she was just five hundred and fifty years old. Though unimaginable to humans, for the *aelfir* this is akin to an adolescent. Many *aelfir* thought her ridiculous, and assumed it was an elaborate joke or work of satire. It was only after the Siege of Korlahsia, nearly five hundred years later, that people started to take her work seriously.

5 The *Drae Adhe* are the *aelfir*'s fearsome scouts. They routinely patrol the forests and protect the boundaries of the *aelfir* kingdoms. Masters of stealth and ambush, the *Drae Adhe* (or 'seeking ones') are legendary among the younger races. *Drae Adhe* is also the source of our word 'dryad', used in Hoim and the Arendsonn Kingdom.

Roin and defended the city of Thea Suin. I have slept on the Salt Flats, fought on Kourgaad Plains and walked among the humans from across the sea.

I am La Darielle Daellen Staern[6] and this is my gift to you.

This is *The* Aelfir *Art of War*.

---

6 'La' is an honorific, usually given to anyone who has served in the King's retinue. There is no distinction between the retinues of the south, north or High King. La Darielle served under High King Fuendil Asendilar during the closing stages of the Asaanic War.

2

philosophy:
the Darkening Way

The lives of men are but as leaves turning with the seasons.[1] The dwarf too, although of longer lifespan, succumbs to the ravages of time. The orc is so mindless of himself that he constantly courts death. Why else does he throw himself into the jaws of battle time and again? Only we *aelfir* can defy the long sleep due to our connection to the land and our communion with each other. As every *aelfir* learns, this near immortality is to be cherished, for we are not invincible: we can be weakened by starvation and slain in combat, just as the younger races are. Our great beauty does not make us invulnerable,

1 The *aelfir* have a strong preoccupation with how short-lived humans are. I often overheard *aelfir* remark, 'Ah, he's still alive then,' each morning when I awoke. It was as if they expected me to pass away at any given moment. Some, less charitable, *aelfir* took bets against whether I could complete this translation before I expired. Such are the entertainments of the long-lived.

no matter how much the innocent and the proud may hope otherwise. For this reason every *aelfir* should be trained to fight, not just to defend the land we hold dear, but also to maintain the rich and endless threads of our lives.

Those following the warrior's path must live with death as a constant companion: a fearful proposition for any *aelfir*.

The temptation to flee the field of battle to preserve the gift of immortality is a strong one, even for the most dutiful *aelfir*. It is for this reason one of our greatest philosophers, Saim Nai Thea Suin, set down a code of conduct called the Darkening Way.[2] Saim Nai Thea Suin taught his students to become one with death's shadow and to stare at enemies with an implacable and unflinching regard.

The first students of the Darkening Way were better prepared for oblivion when facing their enemy at the Battle of Al Silv. The teaching grew in popularity and many agreed the Darkening Way prevented the *aelfir* from being routed at key battles, even in the face of the sinister *Hael Es Haim*.[3] Many of Saim Nai Thea Suin's disciples carried out great acts of selfless heroism, selling their own lives dearly so that the land and other *aelfir*

2 Saim Nai Thea Suin is nothing short of a legend among the *aelfir*. He was a disciple of Khaeris when she taught in towns during the Enlightenment. After Khaeris ascended, Saim Nai Thea Suin departed for Korlahsia and penned *The Darkening Way*. When I asked if he was still alive, the *aelfir* would fall silent and refuse to be drawn on the subject.

3 The *Hael Es Haim* are shadow creatures of the Umber Reach Forest. They are called Umber Wraiths by some human metaphysicians. The *aelfir* I met were unusually close-mouthed about these terrible creatures.

might be spared. All warriors admit that, whilst difficult to adhere to, it is the Darkening Way that makes living with the threat of death tolerable and steels them for conflicts to come.

The following excerpts from a transcription of Saim Nai Thea Suin's teachings, *The Darkening Way*, are the most pertinent, but I urge all students of war to read the full text stored at the Bodhleian Library.

Khaeris haéla na'sehn haim,[4]

La Darielle Daellen Staern

* * *

tHe PRACticE Of tHe ÐARkeNiNG WAY

Each day at the rising of the sun one should wash in cold water and don simple black robes. One should spend time in silent contemplation, meditating on meeting oblivion. All creatures descend into the Great Below when the spans of their lives are spent, and the *aelfir* are no different in this. Cold water is a preparation for death's icy grip. As one's life force slips away, so the heat of the body departs. By simply breathing on the back of your hand you experience the gentle heat of life. An

---

4 *Khaeris haéla na'sehn haim* translates as 'May Khaeris watch over your soul', and is met with the customary response of 'Nei kaer nei saima sehn' – 'and nurture and strengthen you'. To fail to complete the response is a huge breach of etiquette. A shorter, more informal version is '*Na'sehn haim*', which is met with the response '*Saima sehn*'.

aelfir's blood is no different from that breath, but carries a greater essence. To dowse oneself with cold water each morning is a reminder that death could be close at hand, ready to immerse us in the long sleep.

the garments

To wear black robes is to divest oneself of any individuality and shroud oneself in oblivion. *Aelfir* are drawn to decorating themselves with intricate fashions and jewellery of rare craftsmanship; these are manifestations of their inner selves. It is only by relinquishing ourselves, our wants, our dreams, our ambitions, that we can truly live in the Darkening Way. Simply by being in every moment and consciously experiencing every breath we acknowledge death. In doing so we can take the correct action to avoid it with no risk of cowardice or shirking our duties.

The robes of those pursuing the Darkening Way feature a loose-legged garment with five pleats at the front and two at the back.[5] These seven pleats remind a warrior of the seven virtues of the Darkening Way.

Benevolence – extended to all *aelfir*, the young and the weak especially.

Courage – in the face of adversity.

Haélai – watchfulness or awareness.

Honesty – in all matters, but particularly concerning oneself.

Loyalty – to kin, House and Host.

5 These garments are called *El Dilar* by the *aelfir*, meaning 'great and hopeful destiny'. In this way followers of the Darkening Way are clothed in the very tenets of their philosophy.

Respect – for oneself and all others.

Saim – an *aelfir*'s connection to the land.

When practice is finished, be mindful of the manner you fold your *El Dilar*. Be mindful of every pleat and the way you gather and bind your belt. Do not chatter and make banal noise; instead let the insight of your communion with death uncoil within you.[6]

6 Watching warriors meditate together is a unique and powerful experience. The air itself seems to be alive with the implacable will of these graceful students of war. There is also a feeling of deep serenity at this time of morning, one which is unparalleled in human existence.

CONTEMPLATION

To contemplate one's own death is a difficult practice. One might be pierced through the heart by a single ill-fletched arrow. One might be broken and laid low by the axes and hammers of the dwarves. Perhaps you will suffer disembowelment by the cruel barbed spears of the orc. It is not inconceivable to be hopelessly outnumbered by goblins and succumb to a dozen shallow wounds.

Even the frail and stumbling humans have sharp steel that can spell the end for an unwary *aelfir*.[7] It is suggested an *aelfir* not contemplate these things for more than seventy-seven heart beats.[8]

After this spell of contemplation, one should look to one's trappings. Blades should be kept razor sharp at all times. Armour should be in good repair, burnished and oiled. Bow strings should be checked and tested, arrows re-fletched and quivers packed with care. Only when a warrior has fulfilled his obligation to his equipment can he consider breaking his fast. A warrior gains a deeper affinity for the field of battle when putting the main-tenance of weapons and armour before such trivial

---

7 The greatest insult a Saimkor swordmaster has at his disposal is 'clumsy human'. For an *aelfir* it is a matter of deep embarrassment to be described in such a way. When I politely asked if the swordmasters would refrain from using the insult in my presence, they simply laughed in my face and asked me if I'd like to duel. Swordmasters are not the most humble of *aelfir* by any stretch of the imagination.

8 It takes around two minutes for the *aelfir* heart to beat seventy-seven times. This may explain the extended longevity of the *aelfir*, or may be a consequence of meditation. Human hearts have a faster tempo.

concerns as hunger. Death cares not for the empty stomach and thirsty throat; death cares only for the blunt blade, the shattered armour, the snapped string. This is when an *aelfir*'s oblivion rises to meet him.

A Life Lived without hope

The Darkening Way is not the absence of light, but the acknowledgement that death will always cast a shadow over the luminous quality of our immortal lives.

This is never more ably demonstrated than on the battlefield, where death is always just a whisper away. By surrendering the hope of survival we can instead concentrate on the aims of conflict and the purpose of our lives. It is by giving up this hope, this sense of self, that we may move unhindered. Our feet are not mired in the marshes of fear, our strikes not stilled by hesitation, our awareness not dulled by doubt. Those who live according to the Darkening Way need not be encumbered by regret or terror, and are never overcome by confusion.

Aelfir moving as one mind

To give oneself completely to the way is to focus on the needs of those around us. We stand shoulder to shoulder with our kin, defending all *aelfir* without thought for ourselves. Many are the times an *aelfir* has stepped forward to receive a mortal blow that was intended for the friend at his side. Some say this is a mindless willingness for oblivion, but I disagree. Instead, this is the intuition of the Darkening Way: to accept that one might play no greater part in a battle than to preserve another's life. By setting aside our own needs (and the hope of surviving) we become one mind. Just as we see a flock of birds wheeling and turning in complete synchronicity, so we too work in harmony.

* * *

These are just excerpts from *The Darkening Way* and no substitute for the whole. No *aelfir* should be without this seminal text.

WAR AND his RETINUE

Much like the High King, war does not arrive alone, but brings a retinue. Death, fear, guilt and remorse are leashed at his heels like slinking hounds. Certain *aelfir* will tell you that there is nothing higher or more worthy than war, no pursuit more noble, no activity as courageous. The *aelfir* who proclaim these words usually experience their battles from the rear of the field of battle; all too keen to gallop into the midst of corpses once the enemy are routed.

War, death, fear, guilt, remorse. Any of these by themselves would be an excruciating ordeal for any *aelfir* to cope with because we feel so much more keenly than the younger races. True, the memories of slighted dwarves are legendary, as is their stubbornness. It is accepted that the savagery and mindlessness of the orcs is unfathomable to anyone with a semblance of sanity. As for humans, they live bleak lives like faded shadows: their loves, tepid; their anger, merely smouldering; regrets and hopes, unremarkable. We *aelfir* experience lows as black chasms, our highs are as bright as the finest midsummer days. Forgiveness does not come easily to our kind, and yet our capacity for compassion and understanding is superior to that of even the most unusually advanced humans.

How does an *aelfir* not become overwhelmed by war and its cruel concomitants? He adopts a harsh and unforgiving aspect; he becomes more than just one being; he channels the darker impulses of the Chosen of Khaeris into something akin to a mask.

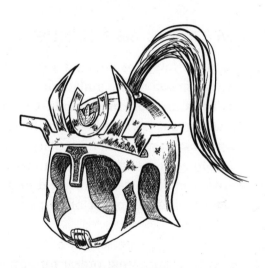

ꞇiirsheni

The helmet of an *aelfir* is more than just a piece of armour.[9] True, it may turn aside the arrows of our enemies but it is not for this reason alone we wear it; the

9 The best translation of *tiirsheni* is 'mind for war'. The literal translation is 'war head', but this fails to explain the full nuances of the term, like so many direct translations.

tiirsheni is our persona writ large on the battlefield. We may share the colours of our House and Host, but the decoration and style will be unique to the individual. No detail is too small to overlook, from the way the metal is burnished to the inscription on the brow. The crest itself is also important. An *aelfir* may opt for a short plume of horse hair or side plates resembling wings. Warriors of centuries past favoured great manes that fell to the waist.

The *tiirsheni* itself is just one part of the ceremony of preparing for war. Some *aelfir* darken their eyes, others darken their whole face. In this way we embody what we are about to become, a dark figure on the field of battle, a solemn and implacable adversary. All mercy is left behind when we darken our faces.

It is a matter of utmost gravity when an *aelfir* has no other choice than to don the *tiirsheni*. Humans may slip on an old cooking pot or leather cap, orcs frequently festoon themselves with skulls, and dwarves encase themselves in plate and chain. There is little ceremony or poetry to these acts. The donning of *tiirsheni* could not be more different. Once war is declared an *aelfir* must contemplate death for seventy-seven heartbeats. During this time, his family will have prepared his armour and his weapons. He then dresses and eats a simple meal before blackening his face and taking up his *tiirsheni*. Once this is done he will address the most senior member of the household, promising to do all he can to protect the world forest, the teachings of Khaeris and the survival of the *aelfir*. Only after he gives his word may an *aelfir* finally don his *tiirsheni*.

This marks a distinct separation from an *aelfir*'s everyday life. Whoever he is, whatever he does, an *aelfir* is entrusted to be of a single mind when donning his *tiirsheni*. The greatest craftsman might be reduced to an archer in this way. No matter. Far better that an archer think of nothing other than obeying orders, turning every moment's concentration to drawing each arrow and sending it to its target. The poet who ordinarily thinks of nothing but words may clear his mind and focus on the swift motions of swing, parry and thrust on the field of battle. Even the High King, whose days are consumed with the intricacies of court, must steel himself and act as one with *aelfir* under his command. To suffer distraction is to be lost.

The act of donning *tiirsheni* is not just a separation from our natural lives. It is a signal to our loved ones. It confirms to our leaders that we are ready. It declares to our enemies that the time for negotiation is past and there can be no respite from *aelfir* aggression.

AFTER THE FIGHT

The *tiirsheni* also allows an *aelfir* to leave some things behind. It shields an *aelfir* not only from the attacks on the body, but also those on the mind. When the *tiirsheni* is set aside, so too are the feelings that come after the battle: guilt at being left alive when others have given their lives; regret for missed opportunities or the failure to act; fear that war will once again darken our existence. As an *aelfir* washes his blackened face he sluices away these feelings, divesting himself of shame and fear. Once the *tiirsheni* is returned to its place an *aelfir* can return to his life as it was before. The poet takes up his quill, the craftsman his tools, the High King continues the duty of ruling and war is remembered, but not dwelt on.

LiFE DURING PEACETIME

For some *aelfir* this disconnect from the experiences of war is very difficult. Their lives are lived in the shadow of combat, their heels constantly dogged by death's hounds. Many *aelfir* manage to find a peace within themselves during the trek home from the battlefield. They share their experiences with their kin and, around campfires, express their fears to those who understand. The physical journey home is mirrored by a spiritual one; it is important that the horrors of war be left at the field of battle.

Once home an *aelfir* can truly be free of conflict. The removal of the *tiirsheni* and washing of the face are usually ceremonial cues to the mind that war is over. Yet war may still occupy the thoughts of certain *aelfir* long after this has occurred. These war-haunted *aelfir* most commonly become Watchers of the Dead.[10]

Others take to the road in search of truths in foreign realms. They journey abroad looking for answers outside themselves, hoping for some respite from their dark

10 The Watchers of the Dead are a regiment of troops that serve all *aelfir*. The Watchers stand guard at Korlahsia, the mountain range where the *aelfir* inter their deceased. The *aelfir* have always interred their dead beneath the mountains to protect them from being consumed by wild animals. Although no *aelfir* said it directly during my stay, there was a strong emphasis on not letting orcs and goblins consume or defile the corpses. The care of mortal remains is a matter of deep importance to the *aelfir*, who believe Khaeris will resurrect them when she returns, and will take them into the stars with her.

thoughts, or a balm to the unsettling malaise in their souls. The wisest of the *aelfir* affected in this way join the Justicar, adopting a deeper spirituality and yearning for justice.

3
ᴛᴀᴄᴛɪᴄꜱ ᴏꜰ ᴛʜᴇ ᴀᴇʟꜰɪʀ

A elfir warfare is primarily concerned with the defence of the ancient forests where we live. We rarely take part in sieges, for such conflicts are protracted and costly affairs, both in resources and morale. Only the dwarves excel at this type of bloody-minded and foolish pastime, being too proud to step down or turn away. One need only study the events at the Siege of Korlahsia to see the wisdom of these words.[1]

We do not raid or hunt other races to extinction either – this is the domain of goblins and orcs. Khaeris herself imbued us with a respect for all living creatures, even those which have no respect for anyone else. Khaeris taught us that the orcs and goblins have as much right to

---

1 The Siege of Korlahsia lasted eighty years. The dwarves beset the citadel where the *aelfir* inter their dead. Many *aelfir* will recount how strength of arms turned the dwarves back time and again. However, there are a variety of factors that contributed to the dwarves' defeat.

live on Naer Evain as we do, even if the Sons of Daellnis wish it was otherwise.[2]

We defend our homes to the extent that anyone setting foot beneath the verdant canopy of the forest pays the ultimate price. Humans and dwarves are particularly determined to savage the ancient trees and for this they must be shown the error of their ways. Occasionally we let one or two trespassers escape so they may spread the message far and wide – the mountains may belong to the dwarf, the plains may belong to the orc but the forest is undisputedly the domain of the *aelfir*.

The Drae Adhe

The *Drae Adhe* are the *aelfir*'s eyes and ears.[3] During peacetime the *Drae Adhe* patrol the limits of the forests tirelessly. This is no mean feat, for our borders are vast and the terrain difficult. Only by maintaining the many watchtowers at the edge of our realm can we keep apprised of our enemy's movements. It is our great speed and our knowledge of terrain that consistently give us the edge over our foes and it is the solemn duty of every *Drae Adhe* to inform the nearest settlement of possible incursion or invasion.

2 The Sons of Daellnis are a group of *aelfir* from the Great Northern Forest still loyal to the first High King. They are particularly distrustful, seeing enemies in every shadow. They consider the lesser races little more than cattle and form a cadre of conservative hardliners unusual in *aelfir* culture.

3 The most famous of the *Drae Adhe* is Suhel Shraykh-Maen, who I met at the Battle of Scarlet Fang Pass. You can read more about her exploits in Chapter 9 of the *Dwarven Field Manual*.

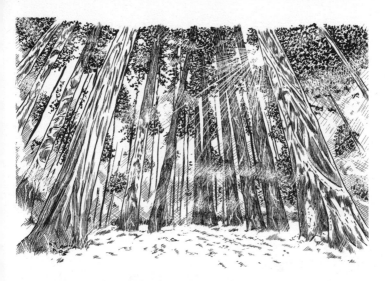

During times of war the *Drae Adhe* range far ahead of the main force, sending fleet-footed messengers back to the general. In an attack, the *Drae Adhe* are used to misdirect and harry the enemy force. They do this in such a way that they suffer as few casualties to themselves as possible. Last stands are generally wasteful affairs better suited to stubborn dwarves and epic poems. All loss of life is regrettable, but every warrior knows his life is at risk the moment he enters service. The loss of *Drae Adhe* units is particularly problematic as they are the lifeblood of an *aelfir* Host.

DRAE ADHE: SMOKE, MIST AND FIRE

The *Drae Adhe* consistently use three tactics to good effect. The first of these is Smoke, whereby they make themselves look greater in number. The second of these is Mist, involving repeated attacks and withdrawals. The last of these is Fire, where they strike at the supply train of the opposing army.

SMOKE

Where more than three or four large units of *Drae Adhe* converge at one time, they may use Smoke to misdirect the enemy. The *Drae Adhe* appear to carry shields, looking like swordsmen. They do this by using swatches of canvas stretched over wooden frames. No *Drae Adhe* in his right mind would allow himself to be slowed by the weight of a shield, so the canvas allows him this deception. It is important to note that orc eyesight is poor. They are easily misled by the crudest of illusions. Dwarves on the other hand are not so easily duped.

On seeing this apparent force of swordsmen, the enemy's first thought will be that they have encountered the vanguard of the *aelfir* Host. Messengers and couriers will be dispatched to the rear to inform the enemy general. Occasionally an orc *Khagan* will lead from the front, but even the dim-witted orcs have an advance guard. Once the enemy leader is made aware of the threat, new orders will be sent and the enemy's deployment will be altered. At this moment the *Drae Adhe* discard their 'shields' and melt back into the safety of the forest or other favourable element of terrain, such as foothills. They then send their own messengers to the main Host as quickly as possible.

The enemy forces will have been aroused, thinking they are about to join battle. Postponement will fray their nerves. The enemy general will also be tested, as he makes the mental shift from readiness to giving orders to standing down again. Repeated use of Smoke wears down an opponent's ability to discern real danger from ruse.

MIST

All *Drae Adhe* are taught how to harass the enemy from afar using the Sight.[4] *Drae Adhe* work tirelessly to intercept enemy forces without being spotted. When the moment is right they unleash several volleys of arrows and then disperse, melting back into the landscape. This by itself does not sound particularly threatening – one unit of *Drae Adhe* versus an entire army is hardly cause for alarm. But consider the impact of some five units of *Drae Adhe* attacking in this way, at different points across the enemy's line, or focused on support troops or the baggage train. Add to this these tactics being used daily in the run-up to the main battle. The enemy is already wounded and demoralised before the field of battle is reached. The enemy general is distracted by needing to deal with the dead and dying, and must manage the frustrations of troops that cannot fight back against this insubstantial force. The wise *Drae Adhe* target enemy leaders and neutralise the enemy army's chain of command. Entire armies have turned back due to the well-placed arrows of the *Drae Adhe*. This is the ultimate in victorious warfare, defeating the enemy without being obliged to commit the entire Host to combat.

4 The Sight is the *aelfir* longbow. A more detailed description is included in Chapter 4 – *Weapons of the* Aelfir.

FIRE

If a unit of *Drae Adhe* should find itself in the midst of the enemy, it is suggested they infiltrate even further back. By trailing the enemy forces from the rear they can attack soft targets such as the supply train. Particularly zealous Host Lords have been known to order the execution of the wounded, who invariably end up at the rear. This is a waste of time.[5] By targeting supplies you disrupt the enemy's ability to function as a cohesive whole. The general has to devote a portion of his thinking to dealing with increasing demand from his troops whilst developing the strategy for overcoming the main *aelfir* Host. Having *Drae Adhe* at the rear of an enemy force during the main battle is intimidating for the attacking army. They will be unsure of what forces lie behind them and thus whether the route of escape is as safe as they would wish. This tactic disturbs humans and goblins, but is negligible against dwarves. It has also been known to confound orcs, throwing their plans into disarray.

SPEARMEN

Spearmen should be deployed on the flanks of an *aelfir* Host whenever the enemy bring cavalry to battle. The spearmen in the Host are much better at fending off

5 For all her severity La Darielle was most insistent that prisoners of war, including the injured, be treated fairly. She extolled the virtue of allowing the wounded and defeated to return to their kin and report the *aelfir*'s victories. More recently, the *aelfir* have taken to ransoming human and dwarf prisoners back to their native lands. However, such an arrangement cannot be effected with the orcs.

flanking attacks from cavalry charges than swordsmen or archers. If the *Drae Adhe* report that the enemy has a large number of cavalry at his disposal, you should instead think about deploying the spearmen in the centre, where they can better deter the enemy. A good enemy general will try to use massed cavalry to smash through the centre of the line and come about behind the Host, sowing discord and chaos among your line. Placing spearmen in front of archers, who fire up and over them into the enemy ranks, will make an enemy general think twice before committing his cavalry.

ARChERS

Leave archers within the leafy confines of the forest wherever possible. The forest will afford them a measure of protection from ranged attacks, and also unnerve the enemy. There is little worse than being shot at by an enemy who is unseen. Oftentimes an *aelfir* Host will not be fighting on the actual edge of the forest but a few miles beyond. In these cases it is worth placing archery units behind spearmen formations, or placing them on terrain such as hills.

Aelfir archers can fire between ten and fourteen arrows every minute. This rate of fire is particularly necessary for thinning out massed numbers of orcs, who frequently attack with odds of four to one in their favour. Units of foot soldiers need to be supported by archers. The hail of arrows will deter all but the most determined of cavalry charges down the centre of your line. Light cavalry and horse-mounted archers can often be turned back from flanking moves that endanger your line. It is

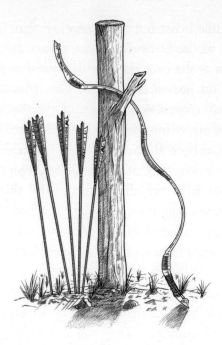

not uncommon for archers to make up half of an *aelfir* host. You will need to be very mindful of your strategy if you find yourself commanding a Host where archers count for less than a third.

Worth reiterating is that most *aelfir* battles are defensive in nature. Arrows fired in great number act as caltrops, and can slow an enemy's advance to a crawl. Lighter-armed orcs are especially vulnerable to arrows and struggle to maintain their morale under such concentrated punishment.

USES FOR CAVALRY

Aelfir horses are the finest in all of Naer Evain – a more noble mount cannot be found among the younger races.

This is no idle boast but simple fact. Before the coming of Khaeris we *aelfir* lived on the plains at the forest's edge, much as the orcs do now. We lived nomadic lives and relied on horses exclusively. Our connection with these proud creatures has not diminished since the founding of our communities among the trees.

Cavalry has been almost unique to the *aelfir* Host. The dwarves are mistrustful of any creature larger than themselves – that is to say all creatures, and this suspicion includes horses. The orcs, who can be relied on never to notice the true value of things, are more interested in the way our mounts taste than the way they handle. Humans alone covet our steeds and pay large sums of money for even a middling example of an *aelfir*-bred mount. Of all the races, it is humans that are coming closest to mastering mounted combat.[6] They are the only race to use cavalry against us in battle, though, as described above, they can easily be stopped using spearmen. This work has been updated to take account of their increasing skill in this area.

Although we *aelfir* no longer use horses in a nomadic life we are indebted to them on the battlefield.

6 This section of the text was heavily revised after the Battle of Century Falls, when human cavalry took to the field against a huge orc Harrowing. Whilst they did not win the day by themselves, they were instrumental in many victories against the orc line. Human cavalry were also present at Fuendil's End, during the closing days of the Asaanic War. The original text had predicted the use of cavalry by humans. I imagine La Darielle was not quiet about this vindication.

MIST FROM HORSEBACK

Archery and horsemanship are truly two fields that are undeniably dominated by the *aelfir*. Using horses as mobile platforms for ranged attacks creates additional worries for the flanks of an enemy's invading force, and can ensure the ravaging of supply trains with impunity. The Sight is a large and unwieldy weapon that becomes more manageable from a mounted position. The ability to redeploy a unit of archers rapidly during the course of a battle is a boon to any Host Lord. The wise *Koraynne*[7] will deploy mounted archers to attack and withdraw, softening the enemy units for the charge by foot soldiers. Mounted archers are also useful at harrying the enemy; see the Mist tactic above. Mounted archers have been known to hunt down units that fall behind or become separated from the main body of troops. Enemy morale is sapped further when expected reinforcements fail to appear.

THE STRENGTH OF HORSES

Heavy cavalry are some of the most terrifying units you can face on the battlefield. Many foot soldiers have told of their great despair when horses charged towards them, trampling them into the mud. The brutal and shocking impact of a massed cavalry charge has turned entire units to rout. Once a rout is under way the panic then spreads

7 *Koraynne* is the military rank equivalent to lieutenant. This role varies widely, from assisting their captain, the *Korasen*, as an adjutant, to leading Houses.

to other units, who fear a similar fate. This forces the enemy general to regroup his forces, instil discipline and re-evaluate his plan.

Expecting dwarves to be put to flight by a massed cavalry charge is about as likely as the sun turning purple. This is not to say that the likely damage that may be inflicted will not justify an order to charge. Dwarves are a hardy and stubborn people and oftentimes you need the ferocity of a cavalry charge to break them at all. Expect to fight to the death once battle is joined. Dwarves know only too well that their legs will not carry them far should they choose to flee.

Where the intimidation of cavalry really comes into its own is against orcs. However, be wary and do not become overconfident. Orcs have their own units of spearmen, and even a dim-witted orc *Khagan* will know how to deploy them.[8] Distract units of enemy spearmen with archery attacks or arcane supplications before committing the full force of your cavalry. Needlessly throwing cavalry at spearmen is wasteful both in terms of resources and the lives of *aelfir* and *E diliir*.

Slashing down from horseback invariably achieves a wound to the head or shoulders of enemy soldiers. This advantage, combined with the relative ease of a solid downstroke, should never be overlooked. So much of the *aelfir* swordfighting styles is focused on attacking the

---

8 '*Khagan*' is the orc word for Great Leader. Orc clans are usually led by the *Khagan*, who is in turn advised by a shaman. You can read more on the complexities of the orcs in the companion tome to these writings, *The Orc Harrowing*.

juncture between head and breast, that it follows there is no better place from which to strike than from a horse.

Having a supply of additional lances and shields also benefits these units, as they may well be required to make repeated attempts on the enemy line.

FLANKING WITH CAVALRY

A general may use his cavalry as a flanking force, especially if he lacks a large number of horsemen. Use the land to hide your intention from the enemy. Dispatch your cavalry a day or two before the main battle is expected, in the hopes enemy scouts will not detect your flanking force. Any chance to attack the baggage train in the days prior to the battle should not be missed. On the day of the battle itself, a previously undetected force of cavalry can cause havoc with the enemy's plans.

In the past, the idea that dwarves could move quickly enough to scout ahead of the main army was laughable. Likewise, the orc suffers from such bad eyesight the very concept of observing the *aelfir* was ridiculous. More recently, however, the damnably ubiquitous humans have served as mercenary scouts for both armies. Clearly the majority of humans are shameless, and will sell their swords even to the uncouth and bestial orcs.[9] Whilst most humans cannot be expected to know true north,

9 Human mercenaries are almost universally despised across Naer Evain, even by the armies who employ them. The coarse and uncouth men of the Arendsonn Kingdom have a lot to answer for when it comes to the reputation of humans.

they do possess eyes and a length of stride that would be envied by the dwarves.

RiiS MAENÁ

Riis Maená form a quite unique unit, although it is not primarily a military one.[10] They have turned their talents to war admirably and have various arcane options at their disposal. You should think of them in the same way you consider archers. They need the support and protection of other close-quarter fighting units, but they are primarily concerned with attacking from a distance. They also need time to make their supplications.

A wise Host Lord should be able to defend his forest without depending on these rare and unusual kin.

The FEW VERSUS The MANY

Even a low-ranking *Korasen*[11] should have fully mastered the units assigned to his command. A leader of a watchtower garrison should be able to turn back a gathering of orcs using the tactics laid down here without recourse to arcane intervention. Many of the most hard-fought battles have not been those extolled in epics, but smaller actions where just a few troops were depended on to turn back vile incursions at the forest's edge.

10 *Riis Maená* are choirs of *aelfir*, called petitioners, led by hierophants. They make supplications to the stars with ghostly songs. I have dedicated more thoughts to the *Riis Maená* in Chapter 8 – *Aelfir Arcana*.

11 *Korasen* is a military rank equivalent to captain. Such *aelfir* frequently lead the Host. *Korasen* means 'strength of the aristocracy'.

4

WEAPONS OF THE AELFIR

We *aelfir* are few in number and our enemies many. The dwarves nurse ancient grudges and resent us for inheriting Khaeris' secrets. It is for this reason that every *aelfir* must be taught the use of weapons, no matter their sex, no matter their age. It is unthinkable that, over the course of our long lives, we should not spend some time in mastering the means to defend ourselves. 'Those that do not fight for the continuation of our kind do not deserve to survive,' was a favourite maxim of Saim Nai Thea Suin. Many *aelfir* confess to gaining significant spiritual enrichment during their training, and it can be that a warrior can find his true self only on the field of battle.

the breath

The Breath is a sword around a foot and a half long.[1]
Some favour a hand guard – this is an overly affected
decoration; a simple crosspiece is all that is necessary.
Just like an exhalation, the Breath starts off wide at the
hilt and tapers to a point. As with all *aelfir* blades, it
should be crafted specifically for the user. Weight, balance and length are all important factors. Using a blade
given to you by a warrior of a similar height is acceptable.
We call this blade the Breath because wielding it should
be as natural to an *aelfir* as breathing. If an *aelfir* should
lose his Breath he will almost certainly be suffocated by
the world around him.

The Breath is primarily a stabbing weapon. If the
enemy is close enough for you to use the Breath, you
should have no problem locating the weak points in his
armour. This is a slender blade, favouring speed and
precision over brutish force. A well-trained *aelfir* can
disarm, immobilise and slay an opponent with only the
Breath as his ally. A slash at the face will cause even the
most hardened enemy to flinch, allowing a follow-up
strike that enables you to lodge the blade in the throat,
or through the heart if the opponent is unarmoured.
Unprotected hands are another target. It is difficult to

1 The *aelfir* seem intellectually incapable of calling an object by an obvious
descriptor. Every word in the *aelfir* language has a deeper meaning and
therefore a confusing and often baffling name. When I explained to La
Darielle that the human word 'sword' simply means 'long, bladed weapon',
she blinked at me and retired to meditate. When she returned, still visibly
unsettled, she asked how I could stand to express myself in such a banal and
prosaic language.

grip the hilt of a weapon if one's own blood makes it slick. The backs of an opponent's knees are also unprotected, as are the gaps beneath the arms.

Breath should never be discarded or left behind. Saim Nai Thea Suin slept with his blade, even in peace time. Some think this fanatical behaviour, yet I say this is something to be aspired to. Warriors seeking to lighten their load on the road to war should forfeit less necessary equipment or enjoy the challenge of bearing this burden. Many are the warriors who have found that when all else has failed the Breath has seen them through their most dire moments.

The Breath is also small enough to be obscured by clothing. This ruse may seem underhand but should not be discounted when facing an opponent who has the advantage of reach or numbers. Should you find yourself disarmed of your main weapon, you will want to sell your life as dearly as possible. If the enemy believes you are unarmed he will become rash, and close in for the kill carelessly. This is when you strike.

Also worthy of note is the fact that many scouts only carry the Breath as their side arm. To carry additional weapons would be to impede their speed. Remember, a scout's greatest value comes from his ability to observe, not to fight.[2]

---

2 *Aelfir* scouts are afforded a great deal of prestige among their kin. Tales of scouts who move like smoke, can disappear in plain sight, climb trees silently and even walk on water are not unheard of. I confess, they are woodsmen without equal, yet I doubt even they can pass over bodies of water without getting wet.

The Spirit

The Spirit is typically a blade between two and a half and three and a half feet long. Larger examples of the Spirit exist but serve better as relics and talismans than actual weapons. Only those possessed of great riches together with little common sense would take one to battle.[3]

The hilt of the weapon is of sufficient length that both hands can grasp it easily although it is often used one-handed. The leading edge of the Spirit is only ever made from the finest steel, bonded along an iron core.

Each one is a work of art, as beautiful and unique as the *aelfir* that carries it. Occasionally an *aelfir* will get it into his head that a blade of pure steel is needed. These *aelfir* should be sent to live among the dwarves, underground in darkness, and made to eat gold. Their thinking is entirely wrongheaded and springs from a ruling class with more money than sense.

A blade of pure steel will be brittle and shatter when dropped or when attempting to parry an enemy's blows. Far better to wield a length of more flexible iron welded to a steel edge. A blade's real strength comes from a

3 This comment caused an absolute outcry when the book was first published. A detractor of the author found a picture of King Fuendil Asendilar bearing a two-handed sword six feet in length. When I asked La Darielle about the veracity of the artist she simply shrugged and said, 'Why do you think he died during the Asaanic Wars? That ridiculous trophy cost him his life.'

combination of the artisan who crafts it and the will of the warrior wielding it.[4]

The gently curving blade of the Spirit favours slashing attacks. The blade's edge should be sharpened at the end of each period of use and the metal polished and oiled with scrupulous care.

Using Spirit, it is possible to sever limbs and decapitate enemies at a stroke where armour is no impediment. Beheading is less easy with dwarves, who seem to lack anything resembling a neck, as is true of the *akuun*; instead attack the knees. The point of the Spirit can be used for thrusts, but this type of swordplay lacks style and finesse. Should you run an opponent through, you may find the blade is held fast by the corpse, particularly by the ribcage. This is a poor situation on the field of battle – only a fool willingly invites fate to disarm him in such a way. Likewise, you should note that orc muscle is particularly dense and has a habit of contracting around the blade whilst the opponent is in his death throes. This takes up time you can ill afford in the midst of a howling melee.

Spirit works well on the orcs, who insist on using toughened hide for armour, which, though light, is susceptible to piercing sword points. However, be mindful of orc *Khagan* who lack the resources for making breastplates but are adept at pillaging them or claiming them during the dividing of spoils.

It is far better to use the Spirit in a two-handed grip

4 It is not uncommon for a sword to take several weeks to be completed. The care and precision *aelfir* smiths bestow upon their blades speaks greatly of their serious attitude to war.

striking at the junction of the neck and shoulder. Remember, even when a blade draws no blood, it does not mean your opponent is not suffering. The shock and force of being struck by three feet of steel and iron is enough to stagger the hardiest of foes, often fracturing ribs or cracking the collar bone. Should you be in any doubt, simply ask a friend to punch you in the throat. Now imagine this pain sevenfold. Extreme, isn't it? The inability to breathe is particularly distressing. Striking an opponent's forearm is also effective and the shock of the blow will still send a weapon tumbling from nerveless fingers should it have failed to remove the offending limb.

Many *aelfir* favour a lunging step towardd the opponent with an upward strike running diagonally across the opponent's body. If he closes with you, he will most likely suffer a grievous wound with his leading leg, immobilising him for the remainder of the battle. If he holds his ground and attempts to parry there is a good chance he will be disarmed or even lose his hand at the wrist or elbow.

Once you have made the initial strike do not hesitate. Great tales are told of heroes who could scythe through enemies like corn. However, it is rare that an opponent will succumb to a single contact. Having launched the initial strike you must follow up with a blow the enemy cannot hope to parry. In this way, you can dispatch an enemy in two fluid movements and not break your momentum. If you miss with the initial strike you have a second chance. Seize it. Having dispatched one opponent you may be tempted to overreach and engage another opponent. You serve not only yourself but your kin by staying mindful of your position in the formation. As in nature, those who stray from the pack rarely last long. A wise warrior is never more than arm's reach from his nearest ally.[5]

We call this weapon the Spirit because without heart and courage we cannot hope to defend ourselves from the ravages of the younger races. The Spirit is not to be worn every day unless an *aelfir* is fully committed to pursuing the Warrior's Art and is a keen disciple of the Darkening Way. Even those *aelfir* who have moved on to a new way of life are encouraged to tend their Spirit and make sure they can be called on at a time of war. It is my hope that one day training will be mandatory and the entire population be able to mobilise should the circumstances call for it.

spirit and breath

Drae Adhe and patrols of more lightly armoured warriors forgo shields and adopt a style of fighting that places the Spirit in the leading hand and the Breath in the trailing hand. This is a difficult style of fighting that requires a special combination of coordination, dexterity and strategy. When one weapon is committed to parrying, the other should be striking the opponent. Many warriors wield the Breath in reverse grip, using it to parry or stab downwards in overhead blows. The Spirit is held point low, one-handed. Fighters adopting this style use

5 This doesn't scratch the surface of *aelfir* swordplay. More can be found in the *Shåine Nai Saimkor*, although you stand about as much chance of getting one of these tomes as surviving a duel with one of its senior adherents.

the shorter version of the Spirit, around two and a half feet long.[6] Saim Nai Thea Suin was inducted into the scouts at a young age and insisted on fighting in this particular style, even after he joined the Watchers of the Dead.

From time to time this style becomes popular in the royal courts of the southern kingdom, despite the fact that carrying the Spirit in public during peacetime is a breach of etiquette and bad form. If younger *aelfir* spent as much time training and caring for their weapons as they did preening in front of mirrors they might learn something useful, should they ever reach old age.

The Sight

The Sight, in my opinion, should be as common to an *aelfir* as the Breath. No weapon we possess gives us such an unequivocal advantage. The Sight is a recurve bow of unsurpassed artistry and the envy of orc and human warriors everywhere.[7] It is made from a composite of lacquered sinew, yew wood and horn. This is an unwieldy weapon, frequently measuring six feet; archers enjoy more mobility and ease of use when mounted on

6 The *Drae Ade* are chosen not only for their ability to blend into the landscape unseen, but also for their strength. It is this strength that enables them to fight with a weapon in each hand.

7 The majority of *aelfir* receive a bow for their thirtieth birthday, if the family can afford it. Those *aelfir* who do not have access to weapons whilst young often embrace diplomatic or arcane skills. However, there is still some stigma attached to not being able to bear arms confidently – another legacy from the *aelfir*'s nomadic beginnings.

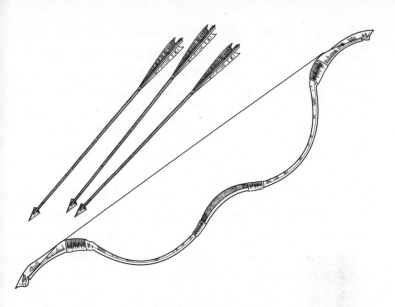

horseback or ranked along a hillside. In battle, Houses of archers frequently line the forest's edge hidden from the enemy, who are more preoccupied with the Houses of spearmen, swordsmen and advancing cavalry. When the enemy approach, the archers may fire with an arcing shot. These volleys, whilst inaccurate on the whole, are deeply intimidating for enemy soldiers.[8] Wind can be a decisive factor, and it is not uncommon for a single *aelfir* to act as spotter ahead of the main group, signalling the strength and direction of the wind.

When battle has been joined, and swordsmen and

---

8 The orcs often refer to the *aelfir* arrow volleys as 'dark rain'. The *aelfir* have adopted this parlance, although no *aelfir* would ever admit to adopting the term from the orc tongue. Seeing an *aelfir* arrow volley is a shocking affair. The sky literally darkens with quarrels, which eventually fall like the rain the orcs so aptly describe. Those troops lacking shields will almost certainly fall casualty, unless heavily armoured.

spearmen are engaged, it will be necessary for the archers to target the flanks. By doing this, they make sure any attempt by the enemy to encircle our forces is subject to a withering hail of arrows. A familiar tactic is to dispatch mounted archers to pick off fleeing stragglers as a matter of course. However, it is good practice to let one enemy escape back to his people, spreading word of *aelfir* superiority.

An added benefit of large volleys of arrows is their ability to hamper enemy cavalry and foot soldiers approaching at speed. An arrow landing point down in the ground is effectively a caltrop, albeit a very tall one. The tail end of an arrow is very sharp despite lacking the steel tip of the leading point. Feet, which are often overlooked by armourers, are easy prey to the dangers of the battlefield. Any general fighting a defensive action and seeking to reduce the enemy's momentum should lay out a carpet of arrows, both for the intimidating effect and the ruin of the opposing army's morale; no one likes to march on wounded feet.

Whilst it would be nice to imagine a bow could be produced and used for a lifetime, in truth it is not possible. The quality and strength of the wood will suffer over the repeated flexing and releasing of the string. A wise archer will have one or even two spare bows at hand for when his main bow eventually tires. The string too can also betray even the most cautious archer, often at the worst time. This never fails to be a surprise and spare strings are an essential part of every archer's equipment.

We call this weapon the Sight because an *aelfir* with

Sight can stop an enemy's progress before the target can even see the danger.

INDIGNATION

An *aelfir* who has not mastered the Spirit sufficiently, or who is aged and past his prime, can always muster Indignation for the enemy.[9] The majority of an *aelfir* Host will be made up of Houses of troops wielding Indignation.

This weapon is over six feet long, with a wooden haft of fine oak at least five feet long. The blade features a curving edge just like the Spirit. The haft is light enough to be used one-handed. However, if a warrior forgoes his shield he may use Indignation with both hands. Competent soldiers can unleash a series of slashing strikes with sufficient range to keep him from counterattacks and ripostes from swordsmen. Some *aelfir* look scornfully upon Indignation, saying it fails to be piercing like the arrow, or as devastating as the slashing blade of the Spirit. This is misguided at best and the mark of an

9 Note, in *aeltaeri*, the aelfir language, the spear is called *staern*, which is where we get the word 'stern' from. However, a better translation of this for the purposes of the spear is 'indignation'. It is also worth noting that 'La Darielle Daellen Staern' translates as 'hopeful one, spear of the north'. Equally it could translate as 'hope and indignation of the north' which sounds contradictory, but makes perfect sense upon meeting the bearer of the name.

overconfident mushroom eater at worst.[10] These *aelfir* would do well to remind themselves that King Korhael Staernsia was a devoted student of this weapon and was never without it. His retinue always carried two replacements for his primary weapon, which is how he gained the epithet 'Three Spears'.

Indignation comes into its own when faced with human cavalry, and has the benefit of reach against orc and dwarf units using hammers and swords. Those wielding it should stand in ranks. The second rank should be arranged to hold their spears through the gaps between the warriors in the front rank, creating a wall of steel points; an unwelcome proposition for any warrior. A House of spearmen arranged in ranks has been able to blunt the force of an attack by cavalry. This is by no means a bloodless transaction, and *aelfir* will be injured or killed if they stand fast. A charge by the enemy gains no advantage at all if the cavalry fail to break through the line.

Every seventy years or so a new upstart *Koraynne* tries to make his mark at the training academy. These insufferable fops invariably declare the days of Indignation are over, and we should embrace the Spirit more thoroughly, taking nothing but entire Houses of

10 Young *aelfir* have been known to ingest mushrooms with certain hallucinogenic properties. This is frowned on by the majority of *aelfir*. It is said orc shamans consume the very same mushrooms to enter into their trances, and humans that do so accidentally think themselves mad or possessed. Dwarves have been known to eat said mushrooms without any noticeable effect. Probably because they're at least half drunk all the time. Hence 'mushroom eater' is a fierce insult in *aeltaeri*, combining 'savage', 'drunk' and 'layabout' in one pithy term.

swordsmen to battle. Should that ever happen I would find it entirely reasonable to paint myself blue and live among the humans, who have precious little sense, but still know the value of a good spear when they see one.[11]

ᗺᕮᖴᎥᗩᑎᑕᕮ

Contrary to common belief, the dwarves did not invent the 'axe', the *aelfir* did. How else were we able to clear sections of the forest to build our homes and our towns? Long before the dwarves saddled the weapon with the crude nomenclature of 'axe', we referred to it as 'Defiance'.[12] Before the *aelfir* gave up our nomadic ways we used Defiance as a tool not a weapon. These versions sported flint heads and were used in gathering firewood. As we mastered metallurgy the axe took on new significance, leading us to the weapon we know today.

Defiance is a two-handed weapon with a haft of four feet, usually made of oak. Defiance is not a weapon to

11 During my six months among the *aelfir* I encountered much talk of 'painting oneself blue'. When I asked any *aelfir* to explain it, they simply looked at me somewhat furtively and muttered that the expression didn't really translate. I can only assume it is a reference to when nomadic human tribes roamed Naer Evain and daubed themselves in blue warpaint. Thus I assume 'painting oneself blue' to be the height of barbarism and low thinking. This was yet another unwelcome reminder that the *aelfir* appear to have more respect for orcs than they do for humans.

12 When High King Fuendil Asendilar ascended the throne he gave the dwarf King Berigunn the Furious an axe as a symbol of the strength and history between the two races. Berigunn returned the axe following the death of his son Killi Temper. This incident led to the 80-year-long Siege of Korlahsia.

give to an unseasoned warrior, nor is it the type of weapon to arm a unit of soldiers likely to be fighting crushed together in close quarters. The backswing of this weapon can break bones just as easily as the intended downstroke. Warriors who are attempting to breach fortified buildings are reminded to keep a heightened awareness of their comrades.

Fighting with Defiance is often written off as a dangerous pastime better suited to more barbaric races, such as orcs. Many *aelfir* assume that Defiance is purely an attacking weapon and of little use for parrying, which is true among those who lack the training. Defiance also surrenders a degree of precision in return for raw punishment. Timing is of the essence with a weapon of this sort, but the payoff is considerable. Where the damage from a sword stroke is transmitted along the length of the blade, Defiance concentrates the force of the attack into a narrower focus. It is for this reason Defiance is good with dealing with more heavily armoured warriors, particularly dwarves. Orc *Khagan* and their retinues are also better armed than standard orc warriors, but still fall to well-placed strikes with this weapon. Such battles are frequently brutish and short, as the orcs will be bearing axes of their own. Strikes from Defiance rarely just wound, but usually kill outright.

5
ARMOUR OF THE AELFIR

Just as there is a weapon for each occasion, so there is a type of armour for each situation. One would not expect a mounted archer to be clad in plate armour, just as it would folly to send swordsmen into battle without a breastplate.

LEAFSKIN

Leafskin armour has been our constant companion since the dawn of the *aelfir* and was prevalent long before the arrival of Khaeris. From a simple sleeveless tunic to a full suit including coif, this type of armour is the bare minimum for anyone embarking on a patrol or joining a Host on the field of battle. Leafskin is made up of many leaves of leather stitched together and is designed to be light. Just as deciduous trees may shed spent leaves, so a warrior can replace portions of damaged armour without a great deal of expense.[1] In our nomadic past, this type of armour would have been reinforced with fragments of bone, a trend that has given way to metal studs.

Leafskin is also used as a primary layer underneath scale or plate armour. It is important the leather be cured correctly and then dipped in hot water. The longer the leather is submersed, the more brittle it will be. Supple leather may afford more movement, but is less protective against piercing weapons. Leafskin will not afford reprieve in the face of arrows, especially those fired from a long or composite bow. The hammers and axes of the dwarves will also render Leafskin useless, as those weapons are concerned with breaking bones, and have no need to pierce the skin.

Some *aelfir* choose to lacquer their armour, which does increase the quality of protection, but you should resist getting the armour waxed. Whilst a suit of waterproof armour might seem a good idea, the reality is less practical. Wax will help arrow shafts to penetrate the armour, as effectively as an unguent would.[2]

A general ordering *Drae Adhe* into a melee with dwarves deserves a scornful epitaph. *Drae Adhe* should

1 It is important to note that *aelfir* are expected to supply their own military equipment. Swords may be handed down from generation to generation, but many *aelfir* will commission a suit tailored to their specific measurements at the first opportunity they get.

2 The *aelfir* are obsessed with unguents, known to humans as ointment. There are unguents for ceremonies, unguents for preventing infected wounds, unguents for making things slippery and unguents for removing stains. The most popular unguent prevents skin ageing and is called Oil of Ó Laie.

only ever engage dwarves at a distance, likewise archers. Messengers also enjoy the protection of Leafskin, enabling them (and their mounts) to move more quickly and tire less. An *aelfir* worth his years will frequently check the stitching of his armour and have the leather treated once a season, lest it dry out and crack.

ÐRAGONSKIN

To deny an *aelfir* his birthright of poise and deft movement is usually unthinkable. It is for this reason that the majority of *aelfir* wear Dragonskin for any major engagement.[3] Dragonskin consists of iron scales sewn to a leather shirt. This adds the additional resistance of metal to the protection enjoyed from Leafskin. Dragonskin is unusual because the wearer does not surrender the range of movement one would experience when wearing full plate, like those idiot human Knights. One need only witness a regiment of dwarves waddling slowly to war to realise that speed and agility are what gives the *aelfir* an edge in the field of battle.

Some suits of Dragonskin are treated to a thin covering of steel. This, combined with the iron plate and the leather shirt beneath, gives a reasonable chance of avoiding injury from orc bows and the inferior arrowheads they craft. The straight-line force of the arrow can still break ribs, but a puncture wound is prevented by the metal scales and the leather beneath. However, orcs have

3 *Draekaoin* – mythical winged creatures who once dominated the land. The same sort of creatures are known as *Daginn* by the orcs. Curiously, the same legends appear in dwarf accounts.

been known to collect *aelfir* arrowheads from the field of battle to use in future engagements – Dragonskin will not protect you against these. In addition, dwarf crossbows, whilst shorter ranged, will always cause casualties.

As with Leafskin, Dragonskin is not much protection against hammers and axes. One needs to be especially mindful of kneecaps when facing the shorter races. Even a glancing blow from a sword or spear can still shatter bones and thus unsettle a warrior's resolve.

SAİMKOR

Saimkor is the heaviest armour and worn only by those units expecting to face the most severe resistance. Expensive and rare, this armour saps the vitality of the wearer in return for protection from sword thrusts and even well-made or pillaged arrowheads.[4]

It consists of a breastplate and a helmet with a face-guard. The rest of the armour is made from heavy plates, just like Dragonskin armour. Nobles and Lords of every rank need to remind themselves that an *aelfir* does not become invulnerable when donning *Saimkor*.[5] Many are the high-born youths who, when taking to the field of battle girded in steel, suddenly imagine themselves invincible. *Aelfir* visiting the tombs of Korlahsia can bear witness that this is not the case.

In order for any movement to occur the armour has to feature joints and hinges; these are your weak spots.

---

4 Plate armour will become obsolete overnight if the orcs ever discover a way to make high-quality steel arrowheads. Their gifts with metallurgy are limited and orcs are more likely to scavenge for *aelfir* arrowheads after a victorious battle.

5 *Saimkor* armour is not to be confused with the Saimkor Sword School. The word *saimkor* itself has many translations, but has connotations of stubbornness, strength and also an *aelfir*'s connection to the world.

Many opponents will forgo strikes at the well-protected chest and abdomen, instead concentrating on the limbs and face. You will need to practise parrying and be on your guard from attacks of this nature. Orcs are particularly drawn to unleash a series of wild attacks. At first these seem as if they are wide of their mark, but the attacks are intended for your limbs, rather than your torso. Strikes to the head, whilst unlikely to cause bleeding wounds, still have the potential for concussion.

Those *aelfir* who think to take to the field of battle wearing their grandfather's breastplate and helm should bear in mind that romantic tradition takes no prisoners. If your newly acquired armour does not fit correctly, then there is every chance it will betray you. Whether it slows you down, or simply offers your opponent access to your vitals, death is never closer than when you are attired poorly for battle. There is no shame in trading heirlooms with the local armourer. If the breastplate has a maker's mark, typically over the heart, then you should get a good price.[6] Armour is just a tool and if a tool is not right for the job you must find another more appropriate one. Those who attach great sentiment to armour usually end up dead long before the armour itself is destroyed.

6 When I enquired why the *aelfir* give their enemies a target to aim for, directly over the heart, La Darielle looked at me as if I were simple. 'Do you not think the embossed maker's mark affords the warrior's heart a greater degree of protection?' she replied. Closer inspection revealed the steel over an *aelfir*'s heart to be thicker by a fifth again than the rest of the breastplate.

NOTES ON SHOULDER PROTECTION

In addition to the face and arms, the shoulders bear the brunt of much punishment during the heat of combat. The different types of armour offer varying levels of protection for the shoulders. Leafskin may feature no protection at all, or what little there is may only be concave pieces of leather, stitched together to provide support for the shoulder joint.

Dragonskin armour incorporates sleeves of scales, often with bracers protecting the forearms. Whilst these undoubtedly make overhead swings and strikes more difficult, this is preferable to spending the rest of your days with a single hand. Or no hands at all.

Lengths of metal hammered into graceful curves, interlocking and artfully hinged, are the peak of our metalworking. An *aelfir* wanting to resist the tide of battle and succeed in turning it back should always invest in shoulder protection when wearing *Saimkor*. Those *aelfir* that do not take shields with them would do well to acquire the heaviest shoulder armour they can afford.

TIIRDILU

In much the same way that Dragonskin features scales of iron and steel sewn to a leather shirt, so *tiirdilu* are items of clothing covering the warrior from ankle to knee.[7]

---

7 *Tiirdilu* translates as 'war foot', another example of how poorly the *aelfir* language translates. *Dilu* belongs to the same root as *dil* (speed) and *dilar* (great destiny). These words stem from the days when the *aelfir* were nomadic. The importance of being able to move quickly and easily has not been lost over time.

However, instead of plates, *tiirdilu* feature rods of metal sewn between two layers of leather.

One method of taking a warrior out of the fight is to rob him of his mobility. Always be mindful of your footwork – be wary of those who feint high, for they will almost certainly strike low. Only the dwarves can be counted on to strike consistently for the legs, as predictably as you expect a dwarf to stop for ale or a misplaced coin. Orcs seem unconcerned about precise strikes, content simply to unleash a great number of blows in a haphazard fashion.

Saimkor worn with *tiirdilu* has significant weight, which makes running impractical. Wait for the enemy to present themselves within striking distance, rather than waste energy by closing with the enemy. When fighting dwarves you will need great patience. Oftentimes closing with the enemy takes longer than the fight itself.

Ciirsheni

The helmet is an invaluable piece of armour and should be checked before every battle. A leather coif is necessary as a primary layer. Some warriors have adopted the ring mail coifs the human warriors favour. Hopefully this fashion will die out, as the human warriors themselves. All an *aelfir* needs on his head is a leather coif and a tiirsheni. This serves as your protection on the battlefield, and also makes you identifiable to your kin. The *tiirsheni* provides, in addition, a persona to immerse yourself in when carrying out the carnage needed to preserve our woodlands and our lives.

A *tiirsheni* of decent craftsmanship will feature a

strong nose guard that will be sufficiently reinforced to turn aside glancing blows. It is this area that the enemy will strike at in order to daze you or cause hesitation. The leather of your coif should be twice as thick at the front, over the forehead specifically, to cushion the blows that are aimed there. A *tiirsheni* which is easily knocked off is useless. Always fasten the chin strap, no matter how hot the day or how uncomfortable you might be.

Shåindil

Whilst not a physical object or garment, it is important to note the true value of *Shåindil*.[8] We *aelfir* are preternaturally quick, sensing threats and becoming aware of danger much faster than other races realise.

When the humans first encountered us, they assumed us malevolent forest spirits, on account of our unmatchable speed. The orcs blame the 'witchcraft of Khaeris' for our swift and flowing movement; their shamans suggest we are not slowed by the natural world in the way others are. The dwarves' movement, like their dim minds, is slowed by thoughts of greed and grudges. In truth, *aelfir* speed comes as much through training and mindfulness as it does through birthright. Every *aelfir* has the facility for graceful poise and unfettered reaction. With training we learn how to move in accordance with incoming threats, sidestepping or weaving away from harm. By being mindful of our enemies and the range of their weapons, we intuitively know when we are most likely to come to harm, and can take action to avoid it.

Whilst *Saimkor* armour may be our most outstanding metalworking achievement, our greatest strength is that which we are born with, the gift of grace and speed. By putting *Shåindil* at the heart of our training we become the avenging forest spirits of legend, evading our enemies' blades like dread phantoms.

8 The 'Pursuit of Speed'.

NAi STEENÉ

Many Wardens of the Host and House Lords will tell new recruits that *Nai Steené* is a folk tale made up to embellish the myths and legends of the Justicar. Tales feature these selfless warrior-mystics acting as body-guards, snatching poisoned arrows from the air in defence of the High King. As an ex-Justicar I invite any Warden or House Lord to fire an arrow at me. They'll only get one chance.

Nai Steené[9] is the ability to take arrows from the air. Only those who have studied *Shåindil* and taken their gift to its zenith will have any hope of mastering this most unforgiving of abilities. There is little room for error with *Nai Steené* and many *aelfir* are wounded and even killed whilst practising it, even with the precautions of blunt and wadded arrows.

The Justicar are few in number, but they have a connection with the land and with their kin that is unparalleled, even by *aelfir* several centuries old. It is for this reason that a Justicar marshalling his training, deep awareness, and mastery of *Shåindil* can avoid death from the clumsy archers of our enemies. It is important to note that even a Justicar has limits; just a handful of

---

9 *Nai Steené* translates as 'taker of arrows'. Any humans claiming they can snatch arrows from the air are either charlatans, drunk, insane or all three. La Darielle did come under fire from a longbow whilst at archery practice one day, but she calmly sidestepped the offending arrow, rather than deflecting it with her bare hands. Whilst this was an impressive feat, I was disappointed that I'd missed an opportunity to witness *Nai Steené* demon-strated by a celebrated practitioner.

archers can take down even the most accomplished Justicar.

Those warriors attempting *Nai Steené* without becoming a Justicar should stop eating fungus, concentrate on *Shâindil*, and purchase a shield.

ḥᴀᴇʟ ᴇʟ ᴆɪʟᴀʀ

Hael El Dilar are the rarest and most treasured of artefacts in all of the great forests and, indeed, on all of Naer Evain.[10] Whilst not armour in the conventional sense, they are circlets of iron and stone that provide a ward around the wearer, protecting him from impure deed and action.

Arrows meant for the wearer break in midair, or shatter from breastplates as if they were kindling; swords grasped for attack suddenly become blunt or stick in their sheaths; fell conjurations fail the caster, often rebounding to cause paralysis or death.

Tales abound regarding the *Hael El Dilar* in every race. The orcs are both fascinated and repulsed by this arcane power, whilst the dwarves lament their own lack of artefacts and covet the objects for themselves. Dwarves refer to a *Hael El Dilar* as a 'Witching Halo'.

The secret of the *Hael El Dilar* crafting was lost with

10 *Hael El Dilar* is often translated as 'Gaze of Great Destiny'. Once an *aelfir* reaches one thousand years old it is said his gaze is so powerful that it can deter 'bad fate' from coming near. Anyone who has experienced La Darielle's displeasure will know there may be more to this than just boastfulness. *Hael El Dilar* is the positive future seen by those with great destiny. Only those with a great and implacable will can defeat the warding effect of those bearing the *Hael El Dilar*.

the death of Queen Surya in the Time of Tears. No one is sure how many of these powerful artefacts exist, only that the High King is entitled to wear one, and three are in circulation among the Great Houses. Others are rumoured to exist in the ruined towns at Umber Reach and in the Scarsfaalen Forest.

6

ADDITIONAL EQUIPMENT OF THE *AELFIR*

As no warrior ventures on to the field of battle unarmed, no soldier should campaign without some certain essentials to provide succour. No matter how in tune with the land, an *aelfir* is still at the mercy of the elements. Only by being more ready than our opponents can we hope to defeat them. Without preparation and planning we cannot hope to turn back the seemingly endless tribes of ever-spawning orcs and goblins, and will falter when tested by the truculent dwarves. Even humans could spell our end if we succumb to complacency. Readiness depends on having and maintaining equipment during peacetime.

CLOAKS OF THE AELFIR

Even the most ordinary of *aelfir* cloaks is far superior to the cloaks of lesser races.[1] It is not uncommon for these items to fetch high prices in foreign markets. Every cloak is made with a lining, usually silk, to help the wearer retain heat in winter and yet remain cool in the warmer months. The cloak itself is made of heavy wool, which keeps the wearer warm even when soaked.[2] Whilst undeniably heavy, the *aelfir* cloak is essential garb for any *Drae Adhe* or warrior taking to the field of battle.

DRAE ADHE CLOAK

A cloak disguises the outline of a person, making the silhouette less recognisable. This is especially useful in woodlands, where the head and limbs of a person make them immediately distinct from their surroundings. Added to the shape-blurring qualities of the cloak is the colour, which also contributes to concealment. Most *Drae Adhe* wear light grey in winter and olive green in summer, making them harder to spot among the varied trees of our great forests. Light grey cloaks are also useful to units who are scouting in the mountains, where they

1 Don't ever expect an *aelfir* to wear anything other than a cloak crafted by their kin. I once made the mistake of offering my own cloak to a shivering *aelfir* maiden. She was aghast, and complained so bitterly that I bought a cloak of *aelfir* manufacture the next day, to spare myself future embarrassment.

2 *Aelfir* hate being wet in much the same way cats do. An *aelfir*'s expression sours considerably if he is caught out in rain. The human expression 'a face like a wet blanket' is derived from describing miserable elves in sodden cloaks.

can rely on the mist to keep them hidden from prying eyes. Orc eyes are inferior to ours, and humans are also less perceptive, further assisting our ability to merge with the very woodlands we seek to protect.

The *Drae Adhe*'s mastery of silent, indiscernible movement is almost incomprehensible to the lesser races. Myths have sprung up of phantom-like *aelfir* who are as ethereal wraiths in the trees, or mortal creatures who wear cloaks that bestow invisibility. Such cloaks do exist, but are far more rare than our enemies imagine.

house cloak

House cloaks differ to those worn by the *Drae Adhe* as they are dyed with the colours of the House the unit belongs to. A unit that serves with a specific Host long term will add a large crest of the House in the appropriate colour. This effectively transforms the cloak from a purpose of obfuscation to one of communication; it becomes a banner that informs the Host Lord of the progress and deployment of his forces. A Lord with good eyesight and nimble mind will be able to count the troops he has under his command, becoming aware of casualties in moments. Furthermore, a cloak bearing a crest will also inform the Host Lord that the wearers are veterans. Likewise, a unit lacking crests will be most likely be new to the Host or untried altogether.

House cloaks have also been pressed in to service to confuse our more perceptive opponents. A wise enemy leader will know which cloaks are worn by which *aelfir* units. Assan Firebringer made it his business to know which colours represented which units; yet another reminder the orcs are not always entirely stupid. Humans, of course, seem baffled by this system, although they may eventually work it out.

A simple but interesting gambit a House Lord can employ is to order his warriors to swap cloaks. Imagine orcs closing with a choir of lightly armed and armoured *Riis Maená*, only to discover they are in fact swordsmen; yet another deception a cunning leader can use to his advantage.

Lastly, and this should never be overlooked, a cloak is a protecting blanket for cold winter nights. Warriors need to be in the peak of health if they are to survive the field of battle; the elements can be as much an enemy as the most bloody orc.

IMBUED CLOAKS

In recent years those most cherished triplets, Morrigah, Badh and Machen Asendilar, have been greatly consumed by the need to provide our forces with artefacts and garments which will ensure our survival and victory over the lesser races.[3] Their ceaseless devotion has resulted in the crafting of wondrous arcane items for our people.[4]

3 I am impressed with La Darielle's moderate tone here. She and Badh have a famously poor relationship. No one knows quite why this is, although some suspect La Darielle's abrasive and direct attitude grates on Badh's softer and more reasonable mien. Others hint that La Darielle has offended the hierophant in some way connected with Badh's father.

4 See also Chapter 8 – *Aelfir* Arcana for detailed descriptions of artefacts and weapons of great power. They are the objects and treasures of epic tales and often works of art in their own right.

The Spider-silk cloak is, at first glance, not something any *aelfir* would particularly want to wear. There is a steely coldness about the garment: it looks as if it would chill the bones of the wearer. The cloak is lighter than its woollen equivalent and, due to the arcane secrets of its weaving, almost impervious to arrows and, indeed, many blades.

The Oakleaf cloak has the unusual ability of conferring prodigious strength on the wearer, making the attired warrior even a match for an orc berserker. The cloak is particularly good at concealment in oak forests during the spring and summer, as one would expect.

The Cloak of Divine Radiance is well known to many *aelfir*, and is often the preferred garment of many hierophants. The cloak is notable during the day only for its silvery sheen and fine embroidery. At night the cloak glows with a calming aura reminiscent of Khaeris herself. This light is particularly good for fending off the predations of the *Hael Es Haim*, and weakens them so they may be harmed by mortal blades.

The Wraithcloak has long been an element of the folk tales and storytelling of all races. Far from rendering the wearer invisible, as the humans believe, they actually bestow an ethereal effect. These cloaks are often reserved for those *aelfir* who serve as messengers to the Court of the High King.

house and host pendants

Every *aelfir* is required to wear two pendants. This jewellery usually takes the form of small, silver-coloured coins

that bear the symbol of the House the *aelfir* belongs to, and the Host they have been assigned to. These symbols provide the *aelfir* with a physical link to the concepts of loyalty and belonging. It is also worth noting that the House pendant is only awarded on graduation from the academy at Naer Khaeris. Serving as a reminder of the training and hardship endured to pass the exams, it is the badge of honour of all those sworn to protect the great forests. The pendants also make the task of identifying the dead easier, should the *aelfir* be separated from his blade, helm and cloak. It is an unfortunate truth that death can render a corpse's identification difficult, especially on the field of battle.

TEARS OF SURYA

These fist-sized rocks resemble finely carved quartz. Many are simply smooth-sided, teardrop-shaped stones;

others are carved into flower heads. Regardless of the design, the stones are always referred to as 'Tears'.

After a minor supplication is sung, the stone glows with a divine and calming light until the following dawn. Those sleeping in the nimbus of a Tear find their wounds less grave upon waking, while those who are uninjured enjoy untroubled sleep.[5] A Tear of Surya is also a deterrent to the *Hael Es Haim*, who despise the light and weaken under the silvery emanation. The Tears of Surya were made by High Queen Surya Lailahlluin herself, and were the last gift she gave her people before her untimely death.[6] Unfortunately, some have been lost, particularly within Umber Reach itself, and others have been misplaced by simple-minded adventurers. A small and well-guarded cache of these items exists at Korlahsia, where the Watchers of the Dead use them to conduct their duties.

The best use for these artefacts is to assign them to a *Koraynne* leading a House, who can then use the stones to

5 I was desperately in need of a Tear of Surya myself when I first arrived in the lands of the *aelfir*. They do not stop singing. Even at night there is some lament or love song being voiced in beautiful if unearthly tones. Whilst impressive at first, this singing does tend to diminish the likelihood of sleep. Eventually I made do with wadding my ears with cheese, which is as disgusting as it sounds.

6 High Queen Surya Lailahlluin was driven apart from her husband by the deception of the royal messenger, Shraine Duinda Dellni. Queen Surya died of a broken heart ten years after she learned her husband had been unfaithful. High King Daellnis Aynnkor abdicated, causing a massive schism between the *aelfir* of *Sia Na Roin* and those of *Thea Suin*. This led to a period of history referred to as the Time of Tears. This story is retold in the tragedy called *The Autumn Nights,* a lavish opera of especial importance.

rejuvenate his warriors at night, as well as fending off any *Hael Es Haim*, should they be tempted out of hiding.[7]

spider-silk rope

Spider silk is a rare commodity. It is found on goblins, and then only in small quantities. It is thought they harvest the silk from their loathsome pets, which they breed for size and temperament.

Whilst of little use on the field of battle, this rope is particularly good for tying up prisoners. It is also of use when creating makeshift shelters and ambushing invading cavalry, should they be stupid enough to ride into the forest.[8] Simply tie the rope at a height of around eight feet and then lure the riders between the trees with some easy target. Be sure to have someone gather the horses, but only after attacking the fallen and wounded riders. Spider-silk rope has the advantage of weighing half as much as normal rope and is also three times as strong.

scroll case

Each messenger and *Koraynne* needs a scroll case to keep orders in. Some Host Lords will carry a map of the battle field with them at all times. As orders and reports come

7 The *aelfir* believe the *Hael Es Haim* feast on their very souls. An *aelfir* destroyed in this way is doomed to become a restless shade. It is for this reason that so much of the *aelfir*'s arcane talents and artefacts are geared towards the production of light and the weakening of these haunting phantoms.

8 Note: Never ride a horse in the forest. At best you'll escape with broken ribs when you are pulled from your horse; at worst you won't stand again.

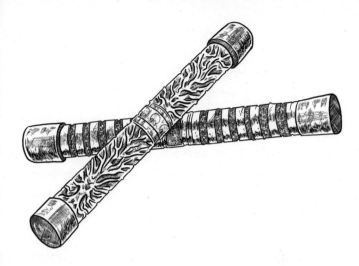

in, the Host Lord can update the map accordingly. Some, however, think that wasting time with ink and quill once the battle is under way is frivolous. Each Lord needs to find his own way of leading, tempered with what he has learned from his superiors. Some Lords are more strategically minded, whilst others are more charismatic and lead from the front. Neither is wrong, and there are distinct advantages and flaws to both styles of leadership.

In my experience, it is always necessary to have a few spare scroll cases on hand, should you need to promote a warrior to messenger.[9] This becomes increasingly likely the longer the battle goes on, as messengers are particularly prone to attracting enemy attention.

---

9 Being 'promoted to messenger' is an ongoing joke inside the *aelfir* military. If a novice shows poor aptitude with a blade and is equally uninspiring with the bow, the instructors will ask if the novice is fleet-footed. 'Well, can you run?' is a favourite taunt of veteran soldiers to the less experienced.

ε ÐiⱠiiʀ (ɦoʀses)

It is a constant hardship that our most faithful companions be so short-lived. Many *aelfir* cannot bring themselves to name their mounts, for when they eventually die the pain of separation is great.[10] An *aelfir* horseman can expect to be served by many mounts over the course of his long span and should do his utmost not to become attached to any particular creature.

In many cases it is not practical to ride the horse you wish to take into combat on the field of battle. Ideally, mounted warriors, and particularly heavy cavalry, would journey on palfreys, whose sole purpose is to provide a means of transport. On arrival, the palfrey would be swapped for a charger, whose attitude, training and build are more suited for fighting.

This swapping of horses appropriate for the task is generally reserved for the Host Lord and his retinue, if indeed they are mounted. Some warriors chafe at this favouritism but the decision is one of logistics, not elitism. The amount of supplies needed to feed two horses for every mounted warrior taking to the field becomes exorbitant.

Fortunately, most *aelfir* cavalry do not have far to travel, as our principal mode of warfare is concerned with defending the boundaries of our forests. Where a

10 Most *aelfir* do in fact have names for their mounts, but pretend otherwise. However, some riders do call their horses by name in public, but they are regarded as eccentric or strangely flamboyant. This is just another example of how important social conventions are to the *aelfir*, and how breaking those conventions will get you noticed for all the wrong reasons.

Host is expected to venture a long distance, such as journeying to Korlahsia, then a supply of palfrey horses becomes a necessity. Rare is one of our funeral processions that reaches the mountains of Korlahsia without need of chargers to protect the mourners from orcs.

bReeÐs

Every House of cavalry will have its own preferred breed. The horses of the Kourgaad Plains are hardy but lack patience.[11] They make good chargers, and have been bred and trained to lead the vanguard of any number of *aelfir* assaults. Selected horses must have great strength and stamina in order to bear an armoured *aelfir*. In addition, they are trained to kick and bite on command and trample wounded enemies beneath their hooves.

The mounts from around Solanhvain are faster and friendlier, and are preferred by mounted archers. Solanhvain horses tend to be blue roans with black tails and manes. The most sought after are those with white dappling, but this is purely an aesthetic choice. Horses that don't respond to training are frequently put into service as palfreys. Those horses that are good as neither palfrey nor charger are sold.[12]

The breeds from Umber Reach are too heavy for warfare and put to better use hauling carts and performing labour. They are variously black, grey or bay with

11 These horses are called *E Diliir Nai Tuesa Tirá*, which means 'great rushing ones of a thousand battles' after the area they come from. The Kourgaad Plains are called *E Hanorothe Nai Tuesa Tirá* by the *aelfir*, which translates as the 'endless grasses of a thousand battles'. I've decided to refer to this area simply as the Kourgaad Plains in the main text for the sake of brevity (and my sanity).

12 To humans. The *aelfir* sell their cast-off horses to 'the lesser races': humans. You may want to bear this in mind the next time an *aelfir* horse merchant starts talking about 'bloodlines and breeding' in order to push the price up. I've since learned I was absolutely fleeced by one pushy and particularly smug *aelfir*.

white stockings. They are most useful for bringing supplies and replacement arms and armour to soldiers fighting far from home. Since the cataclysm at Umber Reach, the horses are harder to find, so maintaining stocks and breeding have been essential in all our settlements.

schooling

The academy at Naer Khaeris is concerned with the training of heavy cavalry, and it is cavalry, along with our arcane brethren, that give us an edge over the orcs. Mounted archers have no central school, and instructors are present at every garrison. This decentralised approach to schooling would be problematic if the instructors didn't rotate around the various towns.[13] Both the archers and those providing heavy cavalry breed and train horses to respond to the leg pressure from the rider, rather than taking commands from the reins. This is important for both types of warrior. The riders of heavy cavalry need to be able to bear shield and lances, then change to a sword when caught in close-quarters fighting. The mounted archers need to be able to fire on the run, or retreat quickly after releasing a volley. Every second it takes to stow a long bow encourages a countercharge from the enemy.

13 Many of the mounted archers can retrace their ancestry back to the times when the *aelfir* were still nomadic. There is a consensus among the town-dwelling *aelfir* that the mounted archers are more coarse and feral than the general population, which is always a cause for friction when they arrive in town.

Most horses tend to be creatures of habit and it is best to train them slowly and repetitively, much as one would a novice swordsman. Positive encouragement has been found to aid the development of good discipline.

BARDING AND EXHAUSTION

The heavier chargers are protected by plates of armour and leather in much the same way as the warriors. This protection covers the head, neck, body and chest. The hindquarters are less armoured; completely covering a mount would risk its total exhaustion. It is worth noting that horses must rest for a greater portion of the day. They can do this whilst standing for short periods. However, a mount benefits most from being allowed a period of hours to lie down, and so enter a deeper sleep. Many myths and legends tell of 'tireless and fearless' mounts, but the reality is somewhat less heroic. Horses actually rest better in larger numbers, as they take it in turns to watch over each other, much as we *aelfir* do.[14]

KEENING STONES (ARCANE)

The Keening Stones, or *Shraine Korá*, are not devices that can easily be taken to war, nor are they reliable, as they require a good strong wind to set off the enchantment.

---

14 The *aelfir* are prone to looking for commonalities with their noble mounts. That horses rarely produce more than one offspring per pregnancy is an obvious thing they have in common with their riders. Human cavalry would do well to note the amount of care the *aelfir* afford their mounts.

The Keening Stones were originally set up all across the *Eanash Shraykh* to confound the various sprites and water spirits dwelling there. Safe passage across that dismal realm was unheard of before the stones were placed.[15] Keening Stones work when the wind catches upon the holes and depressions carved in the rock. It is the wind that creates the high and unearthly mourning sound. This keening confuses more dangerous *es fueniir* and drowns out the din created by the *Bannseedh*.

15 Just as the dwarves are troubled by Ruszalkai, Vodyniir and Ruiir-maidens, so too are the *aelfir*. These water spirits haunt the Freigunn Wetlands and have spelt the doom for many unwary *aelfir*. They are known collectively as *es fueniir*. *Niir* being the word for spirit being. *Fue* is the abbreviated form of *fuen*, which means river, or water in this context. They venture out of the Wetlands and haunt the forest where it meets the river.

The Keening Stones are useful to a Host Lord due to the damage they inflict on enemy morale. A *Korasen* and his Host may well not have to fight at all should they be able to have these stones in place in time for the enemy's arrival. The sound of four or five stones with a strong wind behind them has been known to change the mind of the most ardent foe.

Orcs are particularly familiar with the haunting song of the *Shraine Korá*, and have also suffered at the hands of the various *es fueniir* down the centuries. Interestingly, many orc *Khagan* believe we are in league with the water spirits and they are our allies. Furthermore, they believe that the Keening Stones actually summon the *es fueniir*, and do not repel them, as is the reality of these imbued stones. These simple misconceptions can prove useful at times of duress.

7

the aelfir guide to terrain

For many years, centuries possibly, the *aelfir* roamed the plains of Naer Evain and were not the forest-dwelling people we are now. Before Khaeris' arrival the *aelfir* only ventured into the forests when wood was needed, or shelter sought from harsh storms. It is difficult to imagine those days now; we are indivisible from the land, but particularly the trees. The forests are not just symbolic of our longevity and the cyclic nature of our lives, but can provide the wily general with an ally of substance.

the woodland flank

If the *Drae Adhe* have done their job well, the commanding Host Lord will be alerted to an invading force with time to spare. This respite can be used to deploy the

Swordsmen

Spears

Bowmen

Swords
Cavalry

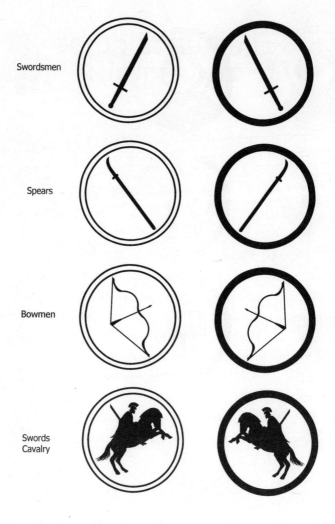

Drae Adhe
(Scouts)

Riis Maena

Command

Mounted
Archers

Host in a way that requires the enemy general to re-arrange his battle line. It is not an easy battle plan to execute, but with suitable training the Host Lord may utilise a tactic I call the Woodland Flank. This tactic can be used without cavalry, but longer deployment times are neccssary. It is most devastating when a Host has a good mix of *Drae Adhe*, mounted archers and heavy cavalry.

The battle line for the Woodland Flank is set out at right angles to the forest's edge. In this way you make it almost impossible for the enemy to flank you on the woodland side. Naturally, *Drae Adhe* excel in this terrain and can make great use of the tactics at their disposal (see Smoke, Mist and Fire in Chapter 3 – Tactics of the *Aelfir*). All your *Drae Adhe* units should be kept in reserve and given orders to flank the enemy under the cover of the trees. Use a hunting horn to signal when they should attack, or use a system of coloured flags if you are concerned about noise and distance.

The rest of the Host need careful consideration. You should order your fastest-moving troops furthest away from the forest, to form the outer flank. Your mounted archers will man the extreme end of the battle line. You will need to keep at least one unit of mounted archers in reserve to support the heavy cavalry. Once the fast-moving units have been deployed you should hold them back briefly. The enemy will be forced to turn his battle line to face yours or risk his entire force being destroyed end to end, one unit at a time. This repositioning will plant a great deal of fear and doubt into the enemy troops. The very idea of being flanked so early in the engagement may cause those of poor discipline to turn tail.

Units of spearmen and armoured swordsmen will naturally be deployed closer to the forest's edge due to their speed. You may even like to deploy your command section within easy reach of the trees, unless you are intending to lead the charge. Make sure your messengers know precisely which units they are to go to and be mindful of how long they will take to arrive.

Just before the enemy has finished redeploying his line you should give the order to the fast-moving units on your outer flank to charge. The enemy units on the outer edge of the line will come under a great deal of punishment from the mounted archers, and fold entirely under the massed charge of heavy cavalry. If enemy units do take to flight be sure to harass them further with mounted archers to stop them reforming later in the battle. Never underestimate the value of continuous intimidation.

With his outer flank in tatters, the enemy general will feel pinned between the edge of the forest, where his troops cannot manoeuvre, and the *aelfir* battle line, which by now will be slanted diagonally. This is the perfect moment to launch a sequence of surprise attacks from the *Drae Adhe* concealed in the forest. If the enemy general is especially naive, he may seek shelter from the cavalry in the forest, in which case he has openly offered himself for assassination. If the general stands his ground, then there is a small chance a committed unit of *Drae Adhe* will be able to attack the command section, slaying key members or causing it to flee in disorder.

Orcs frequently outnumber *aelfir* Hosts, and so we rely on the woodlands to prevent us becoming flanked at both ends of the battle line. Dwarves rarely drag their

portly bodies away from their gold reserves, but should they ever attack a forest you may favour the next tactic instead. Humans and goblins are harder to pin down this way due to their use of fast-moving Grey Riders and cavalry.

the veil of leaves

When an opponent deploys a similar number of troops, or brings warriors of noticeably inferior quality, you should consider using the Veil of Leaves tactic. By hiding part of your Host in the woodland you create the illusion you are outnumbered. This will give false hope to the enemy who will become sloppy and assume victory is assured. It is often the case that an *aelfir* Host is outnumbered, regardless of which enemy we face, so the Veil of Leaves encourages rash overconfidence in the opposing general.

The battle line is deployed in the normal way. However, the archers are deployed in the forest itself and remain seated until a signal from the command section is issued. Although the eyesight of the lesser races is poor, you may like to conceal these units in some way. The *aelfir* cloak is more than sufficient for this job. When cloaks are used in conjunction with the woodlands your archers should remain near undetectable. Meanwhile, the *Drae Adhe* should have scouted ahead and be lurking in concealing terrain, waiting to ambush one or both flanks.

By deploying the archers in the woods you make your opponent assume he has the numerical superiority. If naive, he will become overconfident and rush towards your line, eager to secure victory. If the enemy general is wise, he will become suspicious and advance hesitantly, giving your *Drae Adhe* more time to position themselves. Under no circumstances should you give the order to advance. Let the enemy come to you.

Once the enemy army is within bow range, give the order to your archery units to fire. If you are unable to judge how far a longbow can shoot effectively, you should place visible markers on the field of battle. Have a messenger do this in the days leading up to the battle. The archers should remain hidden if possible, but can emerge from the edge of the forest if the canopy is too dense. At this time you should also give the order for the *Drae Adhe* to use the Smoke tactic, making themselves appear as armoured swordsmen.

Suddenly the enemy will find himself receiving a great volley of unexpected arrows, and threatened on one flank by armoured swordsmen. This sudden change in fortunes will be enough to rout goblins and undisciplined humans. Give the enemy a moment to savour his despair and then unleash a massed charge of heavy cavalry, if you have them at your disposal. If you are limited to foot soldiers then continue to hold firm. Let your archers soften the enemy as he approaches, reminding yourself that even the arrows that miss will litter the battlefield, becoming impediments for the oncoming army.

Do not expend the *Drae Adhe* fruitlessly. Recall them to your battle line once the enemy has begun to flee or to reform. They should most certainly be recalled once the cavalry begin their charge. Remember, the *Drae Adhe* will have been out for three to four days by this point, observing the enemy and reporting back. They will not

have much vigour left and should not be expected to execute large numbers of fleeing soldiers. Their role in this battle plan is to sow confusion and send reports back when key enemy units flee.

If the enemy have brought a high proportion of cavalry you should have your artisans cut long, disposable spears. Do not worry if they lack steel tips, the reach alone will make cavalry attacks against your Host a prickly proposition. Make sure you have enough disposable spears for all of your swordsmen. Spearmen's morale will improve if they too are outfitted in such a way, keeping Indignation sharp and waiting for the close-quarters fighting. Should you have enough time, it is worth embedding these wooden shafts in to the ground itself at a shallow angle, so they point towards the enemy.

ÒUST AND SHADOWS

From time to time it will be necessary for *aelfir* to fight on the plains. Both the Kourgaad Plains and the Salt Flats suffer from an abundance of orcs. The Salt Flats are also home to the occasional giant scorpion. The plains are not to be treated lightly; they are places of dust and shadows where the unwary *aelfir* can quickly succumb. Keeping a strong military presence on the Kourgaad Plains is undeniably important for the *aelfir*. Without a strong and consistent deterrent the orcs, goblins and humans would harass our funeral processions and disrupt our ability to inter our dead at sacred Korlahsia. There are many ways we *aelfir* are superior to the lesser races, and the care of our dead is especially sacrosanct. To this end we must not rely on the forest alone to help us win battles but must also master the plains.

Whilst largely flat, the plains do undulate to some degree and it is the high ground that should be sought at all times. From this vantage point you will reveal yourself to the enemy, but you will also have the advantage of the terrain should he pursue you. High ground also allows the *aelfir* to capitalise on our eyesight, which is extraordinary when compared to the lesser races.[1] You should also send out units of *Drae Adhe* and receive regular reports about the path ahead. The *Drae Adhe* will inform you of any low-lying areas and marshes. Always avoid these as they slow your forces down, lure you to surrender the high ground (such as there may be) and present your Host as a target for ambushes. Your soldiers will thank you too; no warrior was ever so hardy that he enjoyed marching with wet feet. If any of your *Drae Adhe* are late in reporting, you should immediately head for high ground and form up until they are found.

When the enemy reveals himself, you should have a location in mind for your rallying point. It may well be that you are already on high ground, in which case you are to be commended; you will now have additional time to draw up your battle line. The archers will be best served by having increased elevation over the enemy and will need to be screened by foot soldiers.

---

1 One night, I somewhat unwisely explained the human custom of blind people carrying a white staff to the *aelfir* in a tavern. For a moment there was a considered silence and then one bright spark commented that 'Surely all humans are a little blind? Have you seen them shoot?' The tavern erupted with laughter. After that night I found a white staff on my doorstep roughly once a week.

If your opponent stretches his battle line out thinly, then you should consider breaking through the centre with a cavalry charge. If he keeps his line together, then assault the flanks in a series of probing attacks with fast-moving units. Do not engage directly as you will most certainly be outnumbered.

At home we rely on the woodland; on the plains we rely on fast-moving horse archers and supplication to defeat the enemy.[2] The *Riis Maená* will undoubtedly be part of your Host if you are escorting the bodies of the dead to Korlahsia. Make sure they are supported by foot soldiers and within easy reach of mounted archers who can rush to their aid.

The plains present an additional problem to a Host Lord. If your supplies are compromised in any way, your army will quickly lose morale and discipline. The *Korasen* will spend more time dealing with food shortages than keeping watch for the enemy and being mindful of the terrain. It is distasteful to do, but you must forage among the corpses of the defeated enemy whenever you can. It would be easy to assume the foetid and unlovely orcs carry nothing of value, but they require sustenance just as we do. Do not expect a great deal of food from dwarves; they seem more preoccupied with bringing beer to war – which explains their poor swordcraft. Never deny your-self the opportunity to gather additional supplies. Make

2 Supplication is the *aelfir* term for magic. They believe the stars themselves lend them arcane powers. An *aelfir* would never dream of 'casting a spell' as human charlatans claim to do, but instead draws on the unimaginable vastness of the heavens and unwavering light of distant stars.

the unit with the poorest discipline pick over the corpses if necessary.

Supply trains are rarely led by *aelfir* of much military standing or experience. They will slouch and tarry and become a nuisance at the first opportunity. Place your most severe but fair *Koraynne* in charge of the train. Do not assign the *Koraynne* this role permanently or he will lose ambition and become surly. Any wagon drivers with sense will realise that to fall behind the main army is to risk their own lives. They are essentially a moving pantry, and orcs never needed an excuse to raid for food.

8

AELFIR ARCANA

When Khaeris lived among us she taught us many things, but the greatest and most awe-inspiring of these was supplication. The craftsmanship of dwarf artisans is but a weak shadow when compared to the wonders of a heavenly manifestation. Even the shocking, earthy brutality of the orcs pales into insignificance when compared to the terrible destruction that can be wrought by the power of the stars.

Each guiding star is unique to each of the six noble Houses, and Khaeris herself guides the High King and his court. In peacetime, the stars are consulted for guidance. The hierophants and petitioners of the *Riis Maená* commune with these distant benefactors and pass on their wisdom through song and verse. It is said the guiding stars are immeasurably old, even by *aelfir* standards. The guiding stars can guess possible outcomes long before scenarios reach their conclusion. They are the source of the *aelfir* prescience, and the reason we have endured over centuries and survived catastrophe.

In battle, the *Riis Maená* make supplications to the guiding star of the Host and bestow arcane gifts during the course of the conflict. Supplication is achieved through song, using complex harmonies and repetitions of sacred verse, to reach the distant minds of the heavenly powers. The sound of *Riis Maená* singing has been enough to make goblins and humans flee in fear of their lives.[1]

The guiding stars are vast and unimaginably complex powers, even to immortal minds like ours. Once a supplication is made, the choir must wait for the star to consider the request. If successful, the star will manifest its power within sight of the choir. Manifestations are terrifying in the extreme for the lesser races who lack the ability to comprehend this power. The act of singing the supplications and the concentration needed is exhausting, and an *aelfir* Host Lord must urge the *Riis Maená* to use every measure of their reserves. Every casualty inflicted by arcane means is not just a blow to the enemy, but also emboldens *aelfir* morale. Orc raiding parties with weak leaders have been known to rout at the first sign of supplication, a fact worth considering during the opening stages of a battle.

1 There is some confusion among all races between the singers of the *Riis Maená* and the *Bannseedh*. The latter are an *aelfir* myth. Stories tell of female spirits that emit a terrible keening before the death of an important person. *Bannseedh* can appear as *aelfir* women of any age and are escorted by crows. A direct translation of *Bannseedh* means 'woman of the night-time' or 'woman of the long darkness'. A *Bannseedh* appeared to High King Fuendil Asendilar before his death during the Asaanic War. This is retold in the epic poem *Fuendil's End*, one of the greatest works of art created by the *aelfir*.

Light and Gravity

A Host Lord must be familiar with the capabilities of the *Riis Maená* to fully enjoy the advantages they bring. Khaeris taught us much of the heavenly stars, explaining how light travels and how density creates a field of attraction. Light and gravity are at the heart of all the arcane abilities of the *Riis Maená*, our most precious and rare gift.[2]

Supplication is not a precise art. One does not simply call down divine favour on a whim, or expect results in a matter of minutes.[3] Supplications need to be carefully considered and made well in advance of the effect manifesting on Naer Evain. There is also the issue that the guiding star may simply decline to answer the request, no matter how humbly it is asked, or how beautiful the song.[4] Manifestations may take up to an

---

2 This suggests only the *Riis Maená* are capable of making supplications, which isn't true. Even the common folk among the *aelfir* can make minor supplications, called orisons. The most famous of these orisons are the *Drae Solas*, but more mundane among the *aelfir* is *Viirmaenor*, or Treesinging.

3 Also not strictly true. I witnessed La Darielle request a minor version of Halo's Ward, which protected us from the rain, after a particularly heavy night's drinking. 'I can't stand being drenched and drunk,' she said by way of explanation. When I questioned her the next morning she denied ever doing such a thing.

4 I may well be one of the few humans on the face of Naer Evain who has had the misfortune to eavesdrop on a *Riis Maená* rehearsal. They don't always make beautiful music, I can assure you. Hierophants also have a tendency for taking *aelfir* arrogance and dramatics to new and wildly unreasonable levels.

hour to appear due to the great distances involved. Celestial interference can also hamper and deny the most ardent of requests by the seasoned choir.

COMMON SUPPLICATIONS

Solarjaine (Silverlight) – This supplication is one of the most destructive and should be used as a last resort. Some Host Lords choose to use it as an opening attack on the enemy, hoping to gain a massive advantage in morale early on.

The guiding star re-creates a tiny portion of itself on the field of battle, should it acquiesce to the supplication of the choir. Both the guiding star and the choir will be greatly depleted after this supplication has manifested and will need a moment to compose themselves. Witnessing *Solarjaine* is a deeply traumatic and shocking affair. Even *aelfir* soldiers who are aware of what is coming are deeply shaken by the elemental fury of this manifestation. Anything within one hundred feet, friend or foe, is irresistibly drawn in to the manifestation, crushed and incinerated.

No choir in all of history have been able to request this manifestation more than once per battle. The Host Lord must have a degree of insight and be able to predict where the greatest concentration of enemy soldiers will be. This manifestation appears in a designated location and cannot be targeted at an enemy like an arrow. Attempting to obliterate fast-moving enemies, such as cavalry, is almost impossible. However, static objects, such as buildings, are very susceptible.

Korriis (Godlight) – The advantage of *Korriis* over *Solarjaine* is that it consistently manifests much sooner and can be targeted at a formation of soldiers. A beam of shocking white light strikes the battlefield once the choir has made the supplication. The orcs call this the 'sun curse' and with good reason. Those caught under the piercing beam suffer terrible burns and their clothing catches fire.

Orcs, whilst more resistant to the burning effect than humans, suffer from a temporary loss of vision, as they are sensitive to light. A favourite tactic is to blind the orcs with this manifestation and then charge them with cavalry whilst they are too impaired to present spears. *Akuun* and goblins experience a more prolonged loss of sight as they are more nocturnal than their orc kin. This manifestation obliterates the *Hael Es Haim*; even the strongest of them are dispersed for several days. A seasoned choir of *Riis Maená* can call down *Korriis* twice a day if the guiding star looks on them favourably.

Diomhaenteas (Emptiness) – The heavens are not just places of light and darkness, but of matter and emptiness. The vast distances between heavenly bodies are difficult for mortal minds to comprehend. This manifestation fills the hearts of the enemy with a deep and indescribable loneliness. Enemies suffer from a lack of resolve and succumb to a crushing ennui, unable to advance.

This manifestation is a tried and tested way of making humans and goblins disperse in disorder. Orcs are less inclined to leave the field of battle, but will shamble around aimlessly, unable to pick a fight even with their own comrades.[5] *Akuun* are immune to this manifestation, lacking not only the comprehension of the heavens and the trackless distances, but also the very concept of loneliness. *Hael Es Haim* are similarly unaffected.

Tromchiaus (Gravitas) – This supplication requires the choir to sing of past glories and heroic victories of legend. Upon manifestation a chosen unit, typically within a few hundred feet, will be filled with a deep and unshakeable confidence. Soldiers affected by *Tromchiaus* stand their ground like warrior poets of ancient myth, unwilling to give ground even to orc berserkers or the mighty *akuun*. This manifestation is problematic in that the soldiers will not fall back or retreat even if commanded to do so. The compulsion to remain has affected some formations of troops so deeply they refused to leave the field of battle for up to a week afterwards.[6]

5 The *aelfir* are absolutely baffled by the orc penchant for infighting and lack of discipline. That entire units of orcs can simply disregard a *Khagan*'s orders in favour of brawling over 'eating rights' is unfathomable to the *aelfir* mind.

6 Although I suspect the *aelfir* just stood around bragging and complimenting each other on their superior eyesight. And singing.

Tromchiaus is best used on spearmen, especially those expecting to face cavalry charges. Units of swordsmen facing multiple *akuun* also benefit from this morale-boosting manifestation. Although many do not like to admit it, *Tromchiaus* also makes the final moments of a last stand bearable for those about to give their lives. Enemy armies have broken and fallen back when faced with a handful of warriors inspired in this way.

Luan Cosaent (Halo's Ward) – The guiding star reaches down from the heavens and imbues a formation of soldiers with a halo of golden power that emanates from the earth. Some warriors have reported seeing writhing sigils and circles of glowing power marked on the land itself, as if a mighty hand had etched arcane runes around them. This barrier turns aside all but the heaviest of projectiles and slows down enemy soldiers as they charge into close-quarters combat.

Soldiers under the influence of *Luan Cosaent* have described a loss of mobility. Whilst still able to fight, the soldiers find it difficult to advance or retreat at a reasonable pace. This loss of movement is seen as an acceptable trade-off for the increased protection from arrows and javelins. This supplication is a favourite of *Korasen* who strive to avoid the loss of immortal life wherever they can.

Lailah Maen (The song of abundant sunrise) – The choir request the guiding star to turn the full attention of its warmth onto the field of battle. This has the effect of burning off any cloud cover or mist. Orcs, goblins and *akuun* enjoy conducting their raids under cloud or at dusk due to their sensitivity to light. This manifestation can put them at an unexpected disadvantage, because it is also useful for prolonging the day and fending off sunset;

however, it has little effect at night. Host Lords should note this is a supplication that needs to be made well in advance.

This supplication has bought defending *aelfir* an extra day to prepare defences. Some orc *Khagan* are reluctant to attack unless the conditions are precisely to their liking. By ushering in a brighter day, the Host Lord buys more time for his warriors.

Drae Solas (Seeker's light) – This manifestation is so called because the tongues of silver flame it produces are used to light the way by *Drae Adhe*. Most *aelfir* more than a few centuries old can successfully request this supplication; a choir is not needed. Massed *Drae Solas* can cause great confusion at night or early in the morning. Goblins are easily unnerved by these phantom emanations, which they call Hinkypunks. Humans have convinced themselves that the glowing lights are the spirits of people slain by the *aelfir* and refer to the lights as corpse candles. This type of low-level intimidation doesn't work on dwarves who, on seeing glimmers of silver, send for miners and prospectors.

Viirmaenor (Treesinging) – *Viirmaenor* is another manifestation that does not require a *Riis Maená*. It is undoubtedly our most popular supplication and is requested every day of the year, in every town and village.[7]

---

7 During the first few months of my stay I assumed most *aelfir* were simple-minded or slightly drunk on account of gardeners singing to their plants and farmers singing to their crops. This is not the case: all plants flourish when they are the subject of such magic, which is the reason why the *aelfir* always have plentiful supplies of food. It is also the reason forests grow back so quickly after being defiled by orcs or human woodsmen. Trees in the *aelfir* forests are without question the largest and tallest on all of Naer Evain.

The guiding star imbues a plant or tree with gentle and nurturing light, encouraging it to flourish and bloom.

Treesinging has no use on the battlefield to date, although concentrated use of this ability has resulted in almost impassable gorse and thorn bushes. Many minor settlements use these wickedly sharp impediments to deter groups of enemy scouts.

Riisolas Teachtaereachtá (Astral Projection)[8] – With *Riisolas Teachtaereachtá* we have the means of passing messages between different choirs of *Riis Maená*. A choir on the field of battle can report to a choir at the court of the High King, informing them that victory is at hand, or, conversely, that all is lost. No other race has such an ability, and messengers with more earthly feet may take days or even weeks to pass on sensitive information.

This manifestation is undoubtedly our most costly, and only those *aelfir* petitioners or hierophants of the sternest determination and most vigorous health should attempt it. This manifestation places immense strain not just on the individual who carries the message, but on the whole choir, who must keep an uninterrupted vigil for their kin until he returns.

Aelfir lives are not cheap, and every Host Lord must constantly weigh up the needs of the few over the needs of the many. Future losses of life can be avoided by the timely arrival of an important message, but if the choir suffers as a

---

8 *Riisolas Teachtaereachtá* translated literally means 'starlight messages'. La Darielle explained that an individual sends his spirit into the heavens, whereupon the guiding star transmits the messages onwards to a known receiver. This is a deeply traumatic experience, and some starlight messengers don't always survive the process. It is said their spirits are lost in the spaces between the stars; a truly horrible fate.

result they may be rendered useless for forthcoming engagements, such as the following day of battle.

Haimi Dilu (Ghost Step) – Ghost step is one of the stranger supplications and can be requested for the choir itself or a unit of *aelfir*. The singing required for Ghost Step is discordant and unearthly, and not unlike the dirge of the *Bannseedh*. This manifestation renders everyone affected ethereal, and lasts as long as the choir keep singing, although it can take a few moments to manifest. The song itself is particularly difficult for an unseasoned choir to perform successfully and it is rare that any choir manages it twice in one day.

This is an unusual supplication as it allows soldiers to move across the field of battle untouched, until they are in a position to strike at an important target. The sight of an ethereal unit of soldiers also has a crippling effect on enemy morale. Humans especially seem to think the *aelfir* are necromancers, raising the corpses of our ancestors to fight at our side.[9] Ghost Step is also a means of safe passage for a choir who find themselves cut off from the main line. It is this reason that choirs are so difficult to kill, and why so many have escaped when entire Hosts have been slain.

El Hael (Future Sight) – This manifestation allows a unit of soldiers a brief glimpse into the future. Soldiers affected in such a way will be able to accurately guess an enemy's intentions and act accordingly. When cast on archers, this manifestation ensures a devastating and

9 Ethereal troops are one of the more terrifying aspects of *aelfir* warfare. It is for this reason some humans call the *aelfir* the Grey Host. Orcs are also unnerved by these apparitions and call them 'the dead of done-Harrowing'.

unnaturally precise volley of arrows. When an enemy sees this, it is easy for the enemy general to lose his nerve and order a retreat; it also bolsters the fearsome reputation of our archers. If only they were always this accurate.

When cast on a unit of soldiers fighting at close quarters, the effect is equally unnerving. Swords and spears find weak spots in armour, exposed necks are severed, and weapons are sundered from the hands of shocked enemies.

ARTEFACTS OF THE AELFIR

The *aelfir* also possess some magical weapons. Although not available to rank and file troops I note them here out of a sense of completeness. Some of these weapons are relics from the time of Khaeris. Others have been fashioned since by our greatest artisans and imbued with arcane secrets by our keenest minds. The honour of bearing such a weapon is immense, and any warrior trusted to wield one of these great artefacts can be assured that all of history will be observing his actions that day. This alone is enough to bring out the best qualities of a *Korasen*. Each of the great Houses has a historian who records the events not just of the *aelfir* who belong to it, but of the weapons and heirlooms in its keeping. The most famous of these historians is Aynne Kaeri, historian for the High Court.

THE SUN BLADES

Before Khaeris ascended she gathered six of the greatest artisans she could find and had each of them fashion a sword. Into each sword she placed a shard of herself,

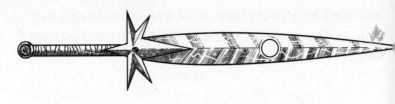

making sure every weapon was of the highest quality.[10]
Each Sun Blade resides with one of the great Houses, and
carries a unique and detailed history all of its own. The
blades are unnaturally strong and retain an edge even if
uncared for. Tales tell of warriors cleaving through three
or more enemies in a single strike. The blades also
embolden the bearer, making him calm in the face of
danger and able to think clearly and concisely. Sun
Blades are entrusted to the *Korasen* leading the Host,
and are a symbol of the authority given to him by his
House. Bearing a blade is a huge responsibility and
allowing such a weapon to fall into enemy hands would
be unthinkable. Soldiers escorting their *Korasen* have
been known to fight against impossible odds to ensure
the artefact remains with the *aelfir*.

Unknown to many, and now thought of as little more
than a myth, was the creation of a seventh weapon: the
Sun Spear. The spear had the unique ability of returning
to the hand of the one that cast it. The spear was last seen
during the Time of Tears, when an untested *Korasen* was
slain in the *Eanash Shraykh*. Some seers predict the spear

10 The *aelfir* make no distinction between the sun and stars. When I
questioned this I was told that 'every star is a sun and every sun is a star'.
These cryptic and abstract responses were commonplace. I asked why the
Riis Maena don't make supplications to the sun. It appears the sun is
somewhat aloof and close-mouthed compared to the more beneficent
Khaeris.

will come back to the land of the living, heralding a new Golden Age of the *aelfir*, but finding an artefact after so long is unlikely.

The Moon Blades

We *aelfir* have had cause to forge new weapons since the catastrophe in Umber Reach. Each of King Fuendil Asendilar's three daughters created three blades that would help fight back against the *Hael Es Haim*.[11] These nine blades have saved countless lives since they were forged.

The Moon Blades were created during the Reunification, after Morrigah, Machen and Badh had foreseen a dramatic vision. The sisters predicted a time when the *aelfir* would need weapons that allowed them to fight during the night-time. Soldiers fighting alongside a *Korasen* bearing a Moon Blade emanate a nimbus of calming light that weakens the ethereal *Hael Es Haim*, making them susceptible to mortal blades.

Although not as powerful as the Sun Blades, the Moon Blades are invaluable in the defence of *aelfir* lives, and

11 The triplet birth of High King Fuendil Asendilar's daughters was greatly celebrated. Multiple births are rare and auspicious events among the *aelfir* and never more so than when of the royal line. Morrigah, Badh and Machen are among the most loved *aelfir* in all of Naer Evain. Each is named after an ancestral figure from the *aelfir*'s earliest myths. All three daughters lead choirs of *Riis Maená* and are often in the vanguard of a Host.

provide a massive advantage to those Lords daring to attack by night. At the time of writing all nine Moon Blades are in the safe keeping of those *aelfir* honoured enough to bear them.

Other blades that mimic the Moon Blades' qualities have been created, but are noticeably weaker than the originals by which they were inspired. Some of these have become lost over time and have since been appropriated by humans.

ANCESTRAL BLADES

Ancestral blades invariably take the form of the Spirit, or sword. An ancestral blade is not simply an artefact that must be kept safe; it is a source of pride, and many are among the finest examples of swordsmithing in all of *aelfir* culture. They are beneficial to morale and the stories of the blade grow with every passing battle, each generation adding to the weapon's legend. They are passed down from father to son as cherished heirlooms, often venerated as much as the ancestors who once wielded them. Losing an ancestral blade on the field of battle is a matter of great shame and warriors will go to unimaginable lengths to ensure their safe return home. Some *aelfir* have been known to lose their lives retrieving a dropped weapon, whilst others, returning home without their blade, can succumb to a madness of shame and regret.[12] The greatest duty an *aelfir* can perform is to

12 The *aelfir* have an unhealthy preoccupation with the concept of madness and enjoy telling strange tales about this condition. The most unusual of these tales is *The Fall of the House of Aiishur*, which is deeply chilling.

return an ancestral blade to its House, should the original bearer fall in battle.

Whilst not anywhere near as powerful as Sun Blades or Moon Blades, ancestral weapons often have some minor enchantment cast on them. Many retain a sharp edge whilst others might glow faintly with arcane light.[13]

MOON STAVES

Each choir of *Riis Maená* is led by a *Naershåin*, or hierophant, who bears a moon staff as a symbol of authority. Whilst each staff is a work of art and adds gravitas to the *Naershåin*, it also has arcane power. Each moon staff is unique, but many have similar qualities and all are imbued with Divine Hope. When the power is requested, all *aelfir* nearby benefit from a feeling of calm and serenity. This should not be regarded lightly; *aelfir* Hosts are almost always outnumbered and this is enough to unsettle our youngest warriors. Should just a handful of soldiers panic and give up their position, the entire unit will be compromised. Fleeing soldiers are not just a danger to themselves, but plant the seed of doubt in every warrior that sees them leaving the field of battle. Divine Hope helps prevent this.

Many moon staves can also summon a great ward of divine light, which stuns orcs and can blind goblins and *akuun*. The light is also an effective weapon against the

13 La Darielle owned a short sword, or Breath, that glows sky blue in the presence of orcs. She gave this weapon to me as a gift the day I departed from *Sia Na Roin* and it has been my most cherished possession ever since.

Hael Es Haim, who must flee or face permanent dissolution.

In conclusion, the *aelfir* dominance over the arcane arts gives us a distinct advantage on the field of battle. In the minds of our enemies we are enigmatic and unnatural. From minor supplications to the mightiest Sun Blade, we confuse and inspire terror in the lesser races. A wise Host Lord will not only use the arcane for tactical advantage but also for the ability to deceive the enemy general. It is these deceptions, these flourishes of theatricality, that allow us to create fear in the minds of our enemies despite our relatively small numbers.

CROWN OF THE HIGH KING

Some items are not available even to the bravest of *Korasen*. These items deserve mention so that all *aelfir* can revel in their splendour; the Crown of the High King is such an item.

The term 'crown' is misleading, as the item is in fact a circlet of purest silver woven into a fantastically delicate plait, set with fine diamonds and amethysts. It is only when the crown is worn that the full extent of its power becomes obvious. The Crown of the High King glows with a light blue halo of divine light. This is the true crown, a manifestation of Khaeris' regard for the *aelfir* and her symbol of care for us.

The Crown of the High King has many powers, and has revealed different qualities to different High Kings over the course of its long history. High King Fuendil Asendilar was mainly concerned with lending his implacable willpower to his troops, so the crown imbued the warriors under his command with an unshakeable faith in their cause.

High King Daellnis, on the other hand, hated the idea of harm coming to his troops. The crown often projected a ward of protection to those under his command. The dwarves, in particular, found fighting Daellnis infuriating due to their crossbow bolts falling short and totally missing their targets.

It would be disastrous indeed should the crown ever fall into the hands of the orcs, who would undoubtedly corrupt it and warp its influence with their malign mores. It is for this reason the royal bodyguard are as much charged with the protection of the crown as they are of the king.

9

hISTORICAL ACCOUNT

*P*resented below is the historical account of Fuendil's
End, as related by La Darielle Daellen Staern. This
battle marked the end of the Asaanic War which had been
waxing and waning for thirty-five years.

– V.

ThE BATTLE OF FUENDIL'S END

The summer of Asaan Firebringer's Great Harrowing was
a dismal one. Too many mornings greeted us with continuous, pervasive rains that washed the joy from the
world. The afternoons were shadowy nothings of over-
cast skies, promising poor crops come the autumn. It was
on the third day of the fighting that High King Fuendil
Asendilar met his untimely end; none of us could have
believed an event so devastating was at hand.

We knew well in advance of the massive concentration

of orcs. The restless patrols of *Drae Adhe* had ventured out from Naer Khaeris, becoming increasingly solemn and gaunt as the war dragged on. What they reported was as shocking as it was horrific.

Asaan Firebringer had assembled an unprecedented number of orc tribes. He'd even managed to lure the goblins down from their caves in the mountains around Voss Colg and the Sun Dog Pass. How many died on the journey across the Salt Flats we'll never know, but if it dampened their thirst for violence it did not show. The assembled tribes swept through the few remaining *aelfir* farmsteads in the west with the ease of locusts. Some ill-advised defensive actions were fought during those grim weeks, leading to many *aelfir* casualties. Worse still the bodies of the fallen could not be recovered, and many fine *aelfir* swords found themselves in the hands of new, unclean masters. The effect of these defensive battles on the enemy was negligible. Doubt grew in the minds of all; many foretold the end of the *aelfir*. Our leaders simply could not conceive of a force so large and had difficulty formulating a way to defeat it. The orcs shambled onwards, an implacable wall of stinking leather and dull, blunt steel, come to grind us into oblivion.

The first day had been little more than probing attacks from goblins mounted on wolves – the Grey Riders. They came at dusk and harassed our defences at night, snickering wickedly to each other in their loathsome tongue. We dispersed them with great volleys of arrows, which rained down on them unseen in the darkness. Those *aelfir* unable to fight behind the city's walls prepared to flee, leaving with little more than the cloaks on their backs.

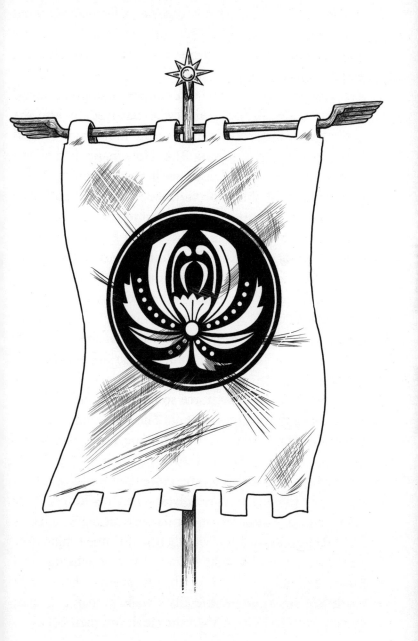

the second day

The second day was as tense as it was tedious. All day long we waited under grey skies and they did not come, not venturing into the extreme range of our bows until dusk. It was as if the goblin shamans had summoned every bat in Naer Evain to provide a pall of leathery wings over their scurrying kin. The Grey Riders supported those on foot, and when the goblins broke ranks, as goblins invariably do, there were stout units of orcs ready to replace them, bellowing and thrusting cruel spears at us. We made them pay dearly for every minute they sullied us with their presence. As night fell we fought on, lit by the arcane supplications of the *Riis Maená*. Our *Korasen* urged us on, entreating us to hold our wall, our *Koraynne* telling us to trust our training. The enemy fled, undone by the unwavering light and purity. The wall around Naer Khaeris remained complete. None had managed to scale it.

When dawn came we stared in horrified amazement at the carnage we had wrought. Orc and goblin corpses littered the field of battle, sometimes collecting in drifts, like volcanic ash. Wolves snarled up at the sky, seeing nothing from their crow-ravaged eyes. The losses were not one-sided; many *aelfir* families were consumed with grief that day upon learning their brightest and bravest had fallen. A hunted look had settled on those of us who had survived, but we said nothing. We thought the orcs might turn back.

Instead the battle intensified.

The Third Day

It was on the third day that I was promoted to serve in the High King's retinue, and so I know better than most how the events unfolded. High King Fuendil had been advised of the situation for months, and had taken a swift boat upriver from Sia Na Roin. Upon seeing the magnitude of the enemy he decided to swell his ranks by an additional three warriors. He knew me by reputation and joked I might turn aside the orc threat with bad language.

The orcs had assembled themselves into something that resembled a battle line, as opposed to the usual ill-disciplined horde. It was clear that an organising intelligence was at work in a way we had not faced before. The orc shamans must have grown in influence considerably during that century.

The Arrival of the High King

Unknown to us all, the High King had been busy in negotiations with the humans at Hoim. His late arrival at the battlements of Naer Khaeris was seen as tardy and uncaring, yet few of us could have imagined the benefit of his actions in the battle to come.

The hearts of even the most sour and cynical *aelfir* were gladdened as their High King took to the walls wearing his silver circlet and bearing his sword, *Arjainshraykh*. The blade matched him in height and had been his talisman during the long and torturous years of the Asaanic War. None could say Fuendil had shunned the field of battle during his reign, and yet his late arrival impacted adversely on the morale of each of us at Naer Khaeris. He did not come alone, but brought with him three choirs of *Riis Maená*, each led by one his daughters: Machen, Badh and Morrigah. Guarding them was his young son, Haélai, who had yet to begin his Justicar training.

We were desperate by this point, resorting to sending out runners at dawn to retrieve arrows from the battle field. Usually goblins pose the greatest threat during the night, though are also known to attack in the early morning. Reclaiming spent arrows was fraught with danger and much of what came back was unusable. Many shafts needed their flights repaired and others had lost their tips. Fortunately, the High King had the foresight to bring full quivers with him from Thea Suin. If it had not been for his presence of mind the battle may well have gone another way.

NUMERICAL SUPERIORITY

By that point the forces of the *aelfir* were much reduced and very stretched. Humans from the Arendsonn Kingdom had attacked us in the east at Khaershåine, dividing our forces. We had also dispatched a number of troops to the north of the Daelluin, in case the orcs assembling at Century Falls should head south and attack the forest. We saw danger in every report that came back, termination in every shadow.

On the evening of the third day of battle we were perhaps some seven thousand archers, and numbered just one and a half thousand men with spears or swords.

The orcs by comparison had forces impossible to count. Some scholars put the figure at thirty-five thousand, others closer to fifty thousand. What is without doubt is that they had three spearheads of *akuun* with them, many carrying battering rams for the gates of Naer Khaeris. Berserkers stalked among their ranks, as savage and hateful as the trolls themselves. We had long been aware that the orc shamans had gained mastery over the trolls but after thirty-five years of war we were surprised there were any of these colossal brutes left.

The River Aids the Aelfir

At last there was some good news. Our scouts reported that Asaan Firebringer had dispatched a portion of his forces to the north side of the Fuenriis river, hoping to find a place to cross either parallel or to the east of Naer Khaeris. The Fuenriis had burst its banks that summer due to a high volume of rain, leaving the southern bank a foetid swamp. Orc and goblin troops who tried to cross succeeded only in drowning. Those few that made the crossing were exhausted by the swim and easily cut down by archers. The orcs and goblins that remained on the north bank were harassed by a few small units of *Drae Adhe* who haunted the Daelluin like wicked *Bannseedh*. Eventually the enemy's morale failed and they fled to the west. There was, however, a far greater threat on the south side of the river.

the Battle Begins

The archers waited tensely, but it was those of us on the wall that had the worst of it. We watched the enemy approach, a vast sea of dark green, hate-filled faces. The wall itself was protected by marshy ground at the north and a patch of rocky ground to the south. This would help deter the predations of three distinct formations of Grey Riders who were now very familiar with our defences. It was at this point that Badh Asendilar and her *Riis Maená* sang the supplications for Halo's Ward to protect the troops on the ground. This arcane boon would help protect them from the black-fletched arrows of the orcs and goblins.

Asaan Firebringer sent the goblins forward again, vast scrums of scurrying, mean creatures under a cloud of infernal bats. The goblins were largely protected from the hail of arrows at first by the vermin in the sky, but even this could not hold back the fierce volume of the archers' endless firing. The *aelfir* foot soldiers waited for the goblins and then signalled for the archers to cease fire. The depleted goblins were no match for the *aelfir*, who dared to stage a countercharge from the gates of Naer Khaeris, led by the High King.

Next came the orcs, their confidence bolstered by three groups of *Akuun*. Machen Asendilar and her choir raised their voices to the guiding stars, calling down the Future Sight for their archer kin. The *aelfir* behind the walls unleashed a punishing cloud of arrows into the orc ranks. The few goblins that remained despaired and broke ranks, seeing their larger kin cut down with ease. The *aelfir* line held and the High King and his retinue led another countercharge, cutting a bloody swathe through the ranks of any orcs who dared approach the gatehouse. The smell of that day was charnel and fell, not easily washed from garments or hair, lingering long in the mind as well as the nose. Fuendil was a silver light in those dark times; orcs faltered when confronted with such steely confidence.

To the south, his son Haélai commanded a unit of spearmen who rejoiced to fight alongside the prince. Suddenly the orcs fell back, pausing to heckle and curse at us in their unlovely tongue. We were elated, but our hopes of an easy victory were dashed immediately. Asaan Firebringer had simply recalled his troops to allow his archers to attack. They had drawn closer and now re-turned a black rain of their own. Our warriors began to fall. Stricken looks were exchanged by the troops on the ground who doubted the wisdom of giving up the protection of the walls. Those without shields were lucky to survive. Undone, we retreated back into safety.

FRIENÒS IN THE SOUTH

As if from nowhere, more arrows sailed down on the orcs' southern flank. Human archers from Hoim had come upstream on barges to lend their aid. This is why the High King had been late: his negotiations with the humans from Hoim had bought us much needed reinforcements. Whilst their range and accuracy were poor, the human archers succeeded in sowing doubt in the minds of the orcs. They still retained the advantage of numbers, but this new offensive caused great disarray to their plans. The second line of the orcs faltered, these extra moments buying our archers more time to cut them down. And yet still the orcs approached in their chaotic way. The *akuun* had now drawn close, bearing tree trunks to smash down the gates of Naer Khaeris itself. Anxiety gnawed at us.

the high king and the akuun

Into this volatile mix came Asaan Firebringer himself. The fearless *Ur-Khagan* led the third wave, keen to ensure the *akuun* were not turned from their task. He towered over his lieutenants, snarling orders with an icy calmness unusual for an orc. A shaman followed in his shadow, whispering counsel and urging him onwards.

The first knot of *akuun* reached the walls of Naer Evain. The High King cast a steely gaze upon them and jumped down from his vantage point. Such ferocious recklessness. The silvery length of his mighty two-handed sword could not be resisted. The trolls lost limbs and were cut down, their fury blunted against the tenacity of the High King's retinue, who stoically refused to give ground. The *aelfir* along the battlements gave a mighty cheer as the first of the *akuun* coughed curses into the mud and died from a series of cuts.

King Fuendil climbed atop one of the fallen monstrosities, as if mounting a hillock, and shouted his disdain at the remaining horde. His shout was returned a thousand fold and we realised we were still vastly outnumbered despite the best work of our archers. It was as if every orc that had ever lived were on the field of battle that day.

ASAAN UNBOWED

Asaan Firebringer, *Ur-Khagan* of the western tribes, and perhaps all of Naer Evain, presented himself, and an expectant hush settled over the armies. Neither of the leaders spoke the tongue of their enemy, but no language was needed. They were going to meet face to face and test the true strength of their resolve. A great roar went up from the orcs and they came on anew, the *aelfir* on the wall bid Khaeris remember them and braced themselves to meet the oncoming tide.

The fighting swirled around the *Ur-Khagan* and the High King, yet none touched them. They were marked out for each other, the ground itself seeming to rock beneath their feet. The proudest and most beautiful of the *aelfir*, the tallest and most brutal of the orcs. King Fuendil had every advantage. The circlet of the High King lent him an implacable mien, his Oakleaf cloak lent his arm great strength, and his retinue were stalwart and unflinching. It was his sword that was his undoing.

Arjainshraykh was long and heavy, even in the hands of one as strong and skilled as Fuendil. He had fought for hours and faced the *akuun* after coming directly from the Conclave of Hoim. That sword, in tired hands, was to cost him his life. Asaan Firebringer cared not for such emblems. He carried a matched pair of crooked blades, called khukri by the human Solari. The orc *Ur-Khagan* deflected grievous blows from his vast shoulders, which were protected by armour stripped from the dead. He shrugged off blows that would have cleaved lesser orcs into separate pieces. That his shoulders were bound up in *aelfir* breastplates will give you some clue as to his size. The High King simply could not land a telling wound.

The *Ur-Khagan* had no such problems, unleashing a flurry of slashing wounds on the King, ripping through his mail, leaving deep cuts weeping royal blood. All about them a similar story played out. The orcs were breaking through, hammering, slashing, cursing, beating at every *aelfir* who dared to stand before them. We were losing.

Asaan caught King Fuendil's sword between his khukri and mashed his armoured head into the High King's face. The King fell to his knees and both sides became silent. Asaan's twin blades were slick with Fuendil's blood and fell like scythes to slash at the King's shoulders. A torrent of blood gushed from the King and he died in wordless shock.

the tide turns

That was the moment the human cavalry from Hoim erupted into the rear ranks of the orc army, sowing panic and discord. But too late for High King Fuendil Asendilar. If the orcs cared that they were attacked on three sides, they did not show it. Still they came on like an irresistible tide, washing up yet more *akuun* at the gates of Naer Khaeris, now spattered with the gore of dozens of orcs and the bright blood of its most dedicated defenders.

We were devastated. The High King had fallen and even the best efforts of our human allies seemed scarcely to stem the tide. Little could we have known that the cavalry from Hoim single-handedly routed much of the fourth line of the orcs.

The fighting at the front was still ferocious and the remaining *aelfir* were grim-faced and sour, preparing to sell themselves at great cost to the uncouth and brutal enemy. An unnamed member of Fuendil's retinue ran forward to retrieve the crown of the High King, only to

find himself facing the *Ur-Khagan*. We thought him lost. Surely there could be no other outcome.

The warrior, armed only with Indignation, parried and blocked the wicked, savage strikes and returned each murderous blow with a careful riposte aimed at the great orc's knees and elbows. It was like this that Asaan Firebringer was whittled down, fighting on even when his thighs were laid open to the bone and one hand had been severed. With a mindless howl the *aelfir* warrior decapitated the Ur-Khagan, then kicked the offending head into the enemy ranks with disgust.

The crown of the High King was safe. The pride of the *aelfir* was untarnished.

the sisters

Whilst both Fuendil and Asaan had met their end, other struggles were occurring to the south and north. The Grey Riders had tried time and time again to gain the upper hand, flanking the forces at the wall and adding to the press of orc bodies. Machen, keen to keep the insult of goblin arrows away from her father's body, directed the archers to cut the Grey Riders down. It is said the howling of spectral wolves can still be heard outside Naer Khaeris to this day.

Morrigah had been working her way along the bank of the river, casting Emptiness on the orcs she encountered, robbing them of their savagery, replacing it with a terrible despair. With the loss of the *Ur-Khagan*, this despair was total, and caused the northern flank of the orc army to collapse. It was here that units of *Drae Adhe* broke through and hunted down the orc shamans. The *Drae Adhe* passed unhindered through the orc lines, which were now a swarming chaos of those orcs too stupid to flee and those shocked at the *Ur-Khagan*'s demise. Imbued with Ghost Step from the *Riis Maená*, the *Drae Adhe* carried out daring raids on the enigmatic shamans. The brave scouts often found themselves at the mercy of the shamans' bodyguards once the effects of the arcane power had passed, rending them corporeal again.

With the shamans dead, the remaining *akuun* reverted to their feral states, turning on their kin. The orc momentum stalled finally, leaving them to the mercy of continued charges from the combined cavalry of Hoim and the *aelfir*.

Naer Evain was safe, the Asaanic War was finally at an end, and High King Fuendil lay dead.

10

AFTERWORD

A SUMMARY OF THE AELFIR

BY SEBASTIAN VENGHAUS

My colleagues,

For a long time now we have likened the races of elves to the northern forest of Daelluin: inhospitable, ancient and unknowable. The elves themselves are like the pine trees they seek to protect: unchanging with the seasons and seemingly immortal; they present a prickly proposition for even the most tenacious of anthropologists. The few facts we have gained about the elves are as pine needles on the forest floor, difficult to digest and uncomfortable.

It would be easy to write off all elves as haughty and unforgiving foes, but this clashes with tales of the elves in the south: wily merchants, graceful performers and artisans of rare talent. Elves have even been known to take human spouses on occasion; hardly the actions of a dismissive and aloof race.

As you are no doubt aware, diplomatic relations between our Kingdom and the elves have improved considerably since the Asaanic War and Conclave of Hoim.[1] The frosty suspicions long held by both sides have thawed considerably. It has been ten years since man and elf stood side by side to turn back the predations of the orc, and yet we still know so little about the elder race.

Not so with this volume. Sent by the King, I lived among the elves (who always refer to themselves as the *aelfir*) for a year. My many misconceptions of this ancient and enigmatic race were questioned, my skill at linguistics challenged, and my very existence hung in the balance on occasion. I found myself immersed in the *aelfir* culture and way of life, and yet I fear I have barely scratched the surface of these otherworldly beings.

Collected here is my translation of *The* Aelfir *Art of War (Aelfir Na Shåin Tiir)*, a manual that is recommended reading for every *aelfir* called upon to bear arms. This is no mean undertaking. Humans are rarely taken to the Forest Kingdoms, and barely tolerated by the northern *aelfir*. That I was allowed to write down this text is testament to the new, yet fragile, spirit of cooperation that exists between our two nations.

I had prepared myself to meet an ancient *aelfir* of intimidating intelligence, one whose charisma and

1 My study of the Asaanic War, *The Conclave of Hoim: Turning Back the Grim Tide*, is available from the University's Central Library and the Kindling Bookshop.

bearing would sweep me from my feet. In truth I was daunted at the prospect of meeting someone who was well over a thousand years old. It was with some surprise that the *aelfir* maiden (who looked younger than me) introduced herself as La Darielle Daellen Staern. War is not solely the pursuit of male *aelfir* it would seem.

La Darielle is something of a living legend among her kin. She has studied all forms of fighting and weapons extensively, enjoyed some notoriety as a poet, served with the *Drae Adhe* and is the only *aelfir* to resign her post as an instructor at the Haimkor Sword School. She has wandered Naer Evain as a Justicar (the implacable warrior-mystic caste of the *aelfir*) and rumours persist that she has shared the bed of kings, spent a decade drunk and even that she killed the orc *Ur-Khagan*, Asaan Firebringer.

Despite La Darielle's many accomplishments (actual and otherwise), she has never risen above the rank of *Korasen*, something akin to our own company captains. I learned that she is famously straight-talking, not gilding her opinion for the benefit of anyone, least of all her superiors. This quality is unusual among *aelfir*, who nurture a strong sense of what is appropriate and diplomatic at all times. A study of their social etiquette would fill this book three times over.

Under La Darielle's keen watch I began a painstaking translation of her seminal text and attempted to learn as much about the *aelfir* as I could. This text has seen various rewrites over the passage of time, being an accretion of her wisdom and experience with arms. It also includes some of the teachings of Saim Nai Thea Suin, one of their most celebrated philosophers. I was given the impression La Darielle was keen for humans to benefit from her teachings and she even proofread parts of the very text you are reading.[2] She often spoke of 'the time of man' and how *aelfir* influence had been steadily waning on Naer Evain.

During this year spent among the *aelfir* I was able to piece together a timeline of sorts. The *aelfir* have a different conception of time, so the dates are approximate only. I admit I am no historian, but I was fascinated to learn of the enmity that exists between the dwarves and *aelfir* following the Siege of Korlahsia. I made some sense of the ruling class of the *aelfir*, long a mystery to human minds. It also became clear these enigmatic creatures are perhaps part of the reason the orcs are so committed to the destruction of all other races.[3]

It would be foolishly optimistic to think we are past our grievances with the *aelfir*. Just as we have many in our fair city who nurse grudges over grandfathers lost in border disputes, so the *aelfir* remember every trespass and blunder into their sacred forests. These old attitudes will not help us unite against the more warlike and unreasonable forces that exist on Naer Evain. Diplomacy must be our watchword, and it would be unthinkable if the regiments of Hoim should ever face an *aelfir* Host in open battle.

2 Thankfully she didn't read the footnotes, otherwise I may not have been returned home in one piece. Or at all.

3 I expand upon this theory in the companion tome to this translation: *The Orc Harrowing – An Oral History*, also available from the University of Hoim's Central Library and the Kindling Bookshop.

This translation alone is a worthy warning to even the hardiest of human warriors that we have much to learn, both martial and philosophical, about war with the *aelfir* and indeed all races. It is my hope we embrace *aelfir* culture and show the elder race we can be trusted in trade, in friendship and stewardship of the land, which they care about most deeply.

Yours faithfully,
Sebastian Venghaus
Anthropologist Royal, Hoim

FiELÞ NOTES OF
SEBASTIAN VENGHAUS

Note: most *aeltaeri* words can be pluralised by adding an á after a hard consonant.

Strangely the *aelfir* do not seem to have the letter 'p' in their alphabet, although they can make the sound, usually when they are exasperated.

The letter 'h' softens the consonant before it in many cases, although spellings of 'ch' are always pronounced as a 'k', and not as the 'ch' in cheese. An 'e' following an 'a' is largely silent and the novice should not worry unduly about making too much of these additional vowels. The speaker should make pronunciations breathy or whispery where a double 'i' occurs, such as in *Riis*.

GLOSSARY

adhe: one, or self.
aélene: sleep. Note: E aélene is the 'Great Sleep', or death.
   Es aélene is a trance.
aélenedil: dreaming.
aelfir: the elven race. This is the singular and the plural.
aeltaeri: the language of the *aelfir*.
arjaine: silver. Not to be confused with *arjain*, meaning

'determined' or *arjainh* meaning 'infant'. A word to be used with utmost caution by the novice speaker.

Arjainshraykh: Determined Wind: a sword reported to be six feet long, wielded by High King Fuendil Asendilar.

asen: proud bearing, aristocratic, of royalty.

aynn: hand.

aynne: grip. Also tenacity.

Aynne Kaeri: A highly respected historian and commentator of *aelfir* culture.

Badh Asendilar: one of High King Fuendil Asendilar's daughters. Badh is the fairest of the daughters, with auburn hair and green eyes. She leads a choir; her speciality is *Luan Cosaent*, or Halo's Ward. She has a famously kind and forgiving temperament and resides at Khaershåine.

baené: beautiful

bann: female

Bannseedh: one of three *Hael Es Haim* who appear to *aelfir* as portents of doom. All three are female and are reputed to sing on stormy nights. They live at the base of the mountains.

Conclave of Hoim (human term): the first meeting of elves and men at the human city of Hoim to discuss an alliance. It was at Hoim that the two races settled an accord and fought together to defeat Asaan Firebringer, the orc chieftain.

daella: north (*daellen*, northern)

Daellnis Aynnkor: High King at the time of the Enlightenment. His name means 'spirit of the north, tenacity of stone'.

Daelluin: literally 'Northern Forest'. The *Drae Adhe* have

a secret training camp here, rumoured to be protected
by sentient trees and shrouded in mist.

daer: hope

dil: speed, or rushing.

dilar: great destiny.

Dilfuen: the river that runs south-east from Voss Kilda
and splits into the Fuenriis and the Suinfuen.

dilu: step; *dilá* is steps, or walking; *diladh* is journey. The
E Diladh is the funereal procession to Korlahsia, a
most solemn undertaking.

Diomhaenteas: Emptiness. This is a manifestation that
the *aelfir* use on the battlefield to sap the enemy's
morale. It is also a term used to describe a spiritual
malaise of those *aelfir* who choose to live on the fringes
of society.

drae: seeking.

draé: seek.

Drae Adhe: Seeking Ones. The *Drae Adhe* are the forest
scouts of the *aelfir*. They are unparalleled among
anyone on Naer Evain as trackers, archers and
ambushers.

draekaoin: mythical winged creatures who once
dominated the land. The same sort of creatures are
known as *daginn* by the orcs.

E: honorific, usually meaning 'great', or 'highest'.

E Diliir: horse. Notice the honorific and that fact the
creature has a suffix pertaining to a person. The
translation at its most basic is 'great rushing ones'.

E Haélai Adhe: the watchful ones, or Justicar as they are
more widely known.

E Hanorothe Nai Tuesa Tirá: the plains of a thousand

battles. Known to humans as the Kourgaad Plains after the human king who lost his life there.

eanash: marsh. *Eanash shraykh* are the Howling Marshes, or Freigunn Wetlands as we call them. The *aelfir* placed tall, singing stones among the marshes to confuse the evil spirits who reside there, such as the *es fueniir*.

ehael: justice, especially when the wrongdoer is killed for his transgression.

el: of the future (positive).

es: of the future (negative).

es fueniir: water spirits. Called Ruszalkai and Vodyniir by the dwarves. Also the Ruiirmaidens that play such a big part in Hoim folk tales. The *aelfir* maintain that all water spirits can foresee the future, and are therefore at one with the future, hence the prefix.

evaidh: the root of the twenty (or so) words for cloak. Please don't ask me to list all them.

evain: land or world. The literal translation from the *aelfir* is 'great forest'.

fuen: river. Also a popular boy's name. *Fue*, the abbreviated form, means water in many contexts.

Fuendil Asendilar: High King of the *aelfir* until the end of the Asaanic War. His three daughters are powerful hierophants and feted leaders of their race.

Fuendil's End: both the battle in which the High King lost his life and an epic poem that recounts those events.

Fuenriis: Divine River. The Fuenriis starts at the point it splits from the Dilfuen and leads to the sea via the area we know as the Nai Roche delta.

hael: anger, or fury.

Haela: furious. Not to be confused with *haél*, meaning 'gaze', or *haéllen*, meaning 'sight or vision'.

Hael Es Haim: are 'ones whose futures are clouded with fury'. This is also the term the *aelfir* use for the Shadows and Umber Wraiths.

haélai: watchfulness, or awareness. One of the seven virtues of the Darkening Way.

Haélai Asendilar: son of the High King, Fuendil Asendilar. Has shown no interest in politics of the court and instead trained as a Justicar following his father's death.

haim: soul or shadow. *Aelfir* tend to use say *el haim*, indicative of hoping for the best for their immortal souls, which they say join with Khaeris in the heavens.

haimi: ghost or 'little spirit', a popular girls' name.

hanarothe: grass. *E hanarothe* is plains.

hasu da: with thanks.

E hasu: formal thanks.

ir: *ir* or *iir* is usually a suffix that simply means 'being' or 'person', hence *aelfir*. The first part of the word *aelfir* is where the root of the human word 'elf' is derived from.

Jaredh El Shurain: a long-lived and popular politician among the *aelfir*. He helped broker the agreement at the Conclave of Hoim and has seen some progress in opening trade links with the dwarves in recent years. His name combines elements of 'determined' and 'young' and might be interpreted as 'enthusiastic and always keen'.

kaer: nurturing, growth.

kaeri: caring one, a popular girls' name. Can also mean 'wind', especially a warm southern wind.

Kaeri Asendilar: High Queen to Fuendil Asendilar, mother of Morrigah, Badh, Machen and Haélai. She died in childbirth. She was considered one of the most accomplished singers of the *aelfir* whilst alive. As a result Kaeri is a very popular girls' name among the *aelfir*.

Kaeri Staernsia: one of the first Justicar. Mother of Korhael Staernsia, a famous hero among the *aelfir*.

kaoin: to weep, or wail. Also can mean 'wind', particularly the north wind.

karnh: a trail marker the height of a man made from stones. Sometimes an improvised burial mound. Can range in complexity from simple stacked stones, to artfully crafted tapering columns.

karnhael: watchtower

Khaeris haéla na'sehn haim: formal and profound greeting.

Khaeris Nai Uaenh, Es Nai Haimi, Asedaer Nai Aelfir: nurturing star of the West, ghost of future time, highest hope of the *aelfir*. It is difficult to comprehend the truth surrounding Khaeris when myth, folklore and historical fact diverge so wildly. The fact that the *aelfir* so universally acknowledge her existence might suggest she actually walked among them.

Khaershåine: the eastern settlement of the *aelfir*. It is home to the Justicar and is the youngest of all *aelfir* dwellings. It is a prosperous and large town due to the generous funding of High King Fuendil Asendilar. Khaershåine means 'the Path of Khaeris', which is fitting for the birth place of the warrior-mystics.

kor: strength of stone, stubbornness. In geography *kor* means 'ridge', or 'rise'.

Korasen: is a military rank equivalent to captain. *Korasen* means 'strength of the aristocracy'. The rank above is *E Korasen*.

Koraynne: is the equivalent of lieutenant and means 'the tenacious stoicism of stone'. The rank above *Koraynne* is *E Koraynne*, the rank above that is *Korasen*.

Korhael Staernsia: a *Korasen* sent to Freed and Al Silv at the start of the Shadow War. His name means 'stone gaze, spear of the mountain'. Korhael is a popular folk hero, and infamous for his bad mood and unsmiling countenance. He went on to be King of the Northern Court and enjoys the moniker 'Three Spears'.

korsheni: an *aelfir* insult for dwarves. It translates most directly as 'heads of stone', but has connotations of dullard, unimaginative and truculent.

La: honorific, usually given to anyone who has served in the King's own retinue. This can be south, north or High King; there is no distinction.

lah: giver of hope, also sunrise.

lah shâin: healer

Lahaynn Suin Na Daer: a *Korasen* sent to Al Silv. Lahaynn went on to become an accomplished hunter of the *Hael Es Haim*. Her name means 'tenacious sun, hope of the south'. She is a famous archer and greatly respected scout.

lai: to be full of, to posses much of, abundance. Also the word for laughter in some contexts.

lluin: forest.

Lluin Na Thea: Forest of the South. This area is home to many *aelfir* living in small communities who survive through a mixture of foraging and raising crops.

Machen Asendilar: High King Fuendil Asendilar's daughter, one of the triplets. Golden-haired and with deep brown eyes, she is the most compassionate of the sisters. She leads her own choir; her speciality is *El Hael:* or Future Sight. Machen often travels around the settlements all year round, seeking out *aelfir* who show promise with the arcane arts.

maen: song.

maena: singer.

maená: singers.

maenor: singing. This word can also mean 'memory' depending upon the context. Although much *aelfir* history is written down, it is only when it is sung and performed that it has real importance. The epic tales, or cycles, are central to the *aelfir* identity, and singers and dancers are some of the most prestigious and lauded members of *aelfir* society.

Maenorfuen: the Singing River. So called because many water spirits would venture along its banks as they travelled south from the northern mountains. It is for this reason many *aelfir* choose to avoid it. More recently it provides a border with the Arendsonn Kingdom.

Morrigah Asendilar: High King Fuendil Asendilar's daughter, one of the triplets. She is raven-haired and blue-eyed. She leads her own choir; her speciality is *Haimi Dilu:* or Ghost Step. Morrigah is the most enigmatic of the triplets and often spends time away from court in the west. Her arrival is not always seen as a good omen.

na/nai: possessive indicator. Nai is the formal version.

naer: woken. Naer Evain is 'woken world' at its most literal. An *aelfir* might explain it as 'the land that is aware of itself'.

Naer Khaeris: the most western settlement of the *aelfir*, and the most martial in aspect. 'Naer Khaeris' means the awakening of Khaeris. In *aelfir* folklore it is the place where she first touched down when she fell from the heavens. The academy at Naer Khaeris trains heavy cavalry, swordsmen, archers and spearmen.

naér: awake or aware. Often used by mystics and philosophers to describe alertness and presence of mind.

nei: and, in addition to.

niir: spirit creature.

riidh: daytime.

riis: from the heavens, heavenly, divine.

Riis Maená: are choirs of *aelfir*, led by singers called hierophants or *Naershåin*. The rank and file are called petitioners.

riisa: star. Important to note that the *aelfir* make no distinction between the sun and the stars. From an etymological point of view the language would indicate the *aelfir* consider sun and stars one and the same, which is frankly baffling.

riisá: stars.

riisolar: starlight.

roin: in archery *roin* is range; in weapons practice it is the reach of a weapon. In travel, *roin* is a measure of distance equal to ten miles.

saim: in woodworking this word means 'quality of

wood'. In philosophy it pertains to an *aelfir*'s connection to the land. When used as a name it means 'strength of the forest'.

Saim Nai Thea Suin: he served as a bodyguard for Khaeris when she visited the various towns during the Enlightenment. After she ascended he departed for Korlahsia and penned *The Darkening Way*. Saim Nai Thea Suin is also called 'The Father of the Watchers'.

saima: strengthen, or the strength of wood.

Saimkor: is the heaviest armour the *aelfir* use, and consists of a breastplate and scale armour on the legs and arms. In this instance the word means 'spirit and tenacity of stone'.

Saimkor Sword School: the legendary school is based in Naer Khaeris and maintains an open door policy to all *aelfir* who find themselves orphaned. A Saimkor Master is a grave opponent indeed. *Saimkor* in this sense means 'connection to the risen land'. It is said some Saimkor masters can run on the very wind itself and leap from rooftops without injury.

seedh: night-time.

sehn: you (*na'sehn*: your).

shåin: a pursuit, or keen interest. Something that is primarily improved by application and repetition.

sheni: head or mind.

shraine: can mean 'yearning' or 'keening' depending on context.

Shraine Duinda Dellni: royal messenger at the court of High King Daellnis and Queen Surya Lailahlluin.

shraykh: howling. Can also mean 'storm' or 'gale' when proceeded by the prefix *el*.

sia: spire, or mountain. *Haelasia* is volcano, or 'furious mountain'.

Sia Na Roin: Spire's Reach, the home of the northern elves. Essentially three large towns based around the foothills of the mountains. These *aelfir* are among the most proud and most isolated. They are not well disposed towards outsiders.

solanh: can mean 'east' or 'death' depending on context. If an *aelfir* has died then the words are *e solanh*.

solanhshåine: is sunset, or 'mourning way of light', which is another *aelfir* term for death.

Solanhvain: the east forest we know as the Arendhavn.

solas: light, especially daylight.

staern: spear.

staernshåin: spearman.

steené: arrow.

steenshåin: archer.

suin: south, or 'of the south' when used as a name.

Suin Fuen: simply 'south river'. It splits from the Dilfuen and continues to the south-east, where it passes through the human settlements of Tour, Hoim, Anghoul and Aurilem.

Surya Lailahlluin: the High Queen during the years that Khaeris walked among the *aelfir*. *Lailahlluin* translates as 'laughter of the woods'.

teachtaereacht: message.

teachtaereachtá: messages.

Thea Suin: the largest *aelfir* city and home of the southern *aelfir* royal court. Considered a seat of learning a gathering place of great minds.

tiir: war

tiirshåin: warrior.

tiirshåiná: warriors.

tiré: battle.

tirá: battles.

uaenh: pronounced 'oo-when'. *Uaenh* can mean west or birth depending on context.

Uaenhshraykh: the wind from the west.

vain: forest

Vain Na Hael Es Haim: forest of the umber wraiths. Note the *aelfir* do not refer to the forest as Umber Reach; this is the usage of the people of Hoim.

viir: tree.

viirá: trees. (*Siaviir*: evergreen, *aéleviir*: deciduous tree, *bannviir*: fruit trees.)

V*iirmaenor*: Treesinging. A type of nature magic that encourages plants to grow quickly, particularly trees.

viirshåin: gardener or 'guardian of forests'.